WINTER

A SURREAL STORIES COLLECTION

DEAN WESLEY SMITH

Winter
Copyright © 2024 by Dean Wesley Smith
Published by WMG Publishing
Cover and layout copyright © 2024 by WMG Publishing
Cover design by Stephanie Writt/WMG Publishing
Cover art copyright © DPimage/Depositphotos

ISBN-13 (trade paperback): 978-1-56146-962-8
ISBN-13 (hardcover): 978-1-56146-963-5

Due to limitations of space, expanded copyright information can be found at the end of this volume.

This book is licensed for your personal enjoyment only. All rights reserved. This is a work of fiction. All characters and events portrayed in this book are fictional, and any resemblance to real people or incidents is purely coincidental. This book, or parts thereof, may not be reproduced in any form without permission.

ALSO BY DEAN WESLEY SMITH

COLD POKER GANG

Kill Game

Cold Call

Calling Dead

Bad Beat

Dead Hand

Freezeout

Ace High

Burn Card

Heads Up

Ring Game

Bottom Pair

Case Card

THE POKER BOY UNIVERSE

Poker Boy

The Slots of Saturn: A Poker Boy Novel

They're Back: A Poker Boy Short Novel

Luck Be Ladies: A Poker Boy Collection

Playing a Hunch: A Poker Boy Collection

A Poker Boy Christmas: A Poker Boy Collection

Ghost of a Chance

The Poker Chip: A Ghost of a Chance Novel

The Christmas Gift: A Ghost of a Chance Novel

The Free Meal: A Ghost of a Chance Novel

The Cop Car: A Ghost of a Chance Novella

The Deep Sunset: A Ghost of a Chance Novel

Marble Grant

The First Year: A Marble Grant Novel

Time for Cool Madness: Six Crazy Marble Grant Stories

Pakhet Jones

The Big Tom: A Packet Jones Short Novel

Big Eyes: A Packet Jones Short Novel

THUNDER MOUNTAIN

Thunder Mountain

Monumental Summit

Avalanche Creek

The Edwards Mansion

Lake Roosevelt

Warm Springs

Melody Ridge

Grapevine Springs

The Idanha Hotel

The Taft Ranch

Tombstone Canyon

Dry Creek Crossing

Hot Springs Meadow

Green Valley

SEEDERS UNIVERSE

Dust and Kisses: A Seeders Universe Prequel Novel

Against Time

Sector Justice

Morning Song

The High Edge

Star Mist

Star Rain

Star Fall

Starburst

Rescue Two

CONTENTS

Introduction   xi
It All Might Be Seasonable

A Long Way Down   1
A Brush With Intent   15
A Home For The Books   23
Kill for a Statistic   39
To Remember a Single Minute   51
A Song For The Old Memory   61
Call Me Unfixable   73
The Man Who Used Shrill Whispers   97
An Obscene Crime Against Passion   111
They Were Divided by Cold Debt   129

Newsletter sign-up   145
About the Author   147
Expanded Copyright Information   149

WINTER

INTRODUCTION
IT ALL MIGHT BE SEASONABLE

For years and years, actually decades and decades, I kept saying that one day I would do a Bryant Street collection or two, and I just never got around to it.

Finally, in the winter of 2023, I decided it was time and told the fine folks at WMG Publishing I was going to do this. Stephanie Writt came up with the cool street-sign logo and I was off.

I thought it would be cool to have Bryant Street be a television series with four seasons of ten episodes each season. (For those of you who don't know, a short story usually has enough story for a single thirty-minute episode of anything on television.)

So I sent the idea of four seasons to Stephanie at WMG and back comes the four wonderful covers using seasons of the year. I was about to object when it dawned on me that four seasons of the year would be a lot easier to explain than four seasons of a television show.

And these would act as ten episodes of a season, but each season would start on the first day of the named season. A full year of Bryant Street.

So I started with the forty stories together and then put them into seasons.

Often a story is set in the title season. Or the story is dark like winter. Or hot like summer.

Or a character in the last days of their lives like winter, or fading like fall. In one way or another, all the stories fit into a season.

But think of them like ten episodes per run. The winter season run, the spring season run, and so on.

Sort of like ten episodes per season of a series like *The Twilight Zone* television series used to be. Every episode different, yet every episode set on Bryant Street.

USA *Today* Bestselling Writer
DEAN WESLEY SMITH

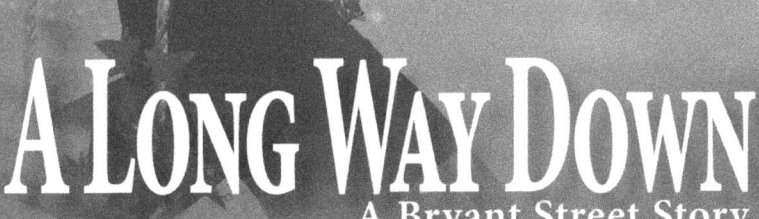

A LONG WAY DOWN
A Bryant Street Story

A LONG WAY DOWN

Lacey Temlin hated her husband. She called him Dead Man. He cheated on her. She waited and watched.

Her plan to kill him seemed perfect.

Lacey needed everything to always be perfect.

Until it became clear they lived in the twisted world of Bryant Street.

Nude, standing in the center of her kitchen, Lacey Temlin let the lukewarm and slightly bitter taste of her morning coffee settle her nerves. She drank it black, no cream or sugar to mar the desired taste. But now the coffee had sat too long after she had made it. It was the only thing not perfect around her at the moment.

Her modern, light granite kitchen counters shone with a polish she doubted they had when installed. The dark tile floors were like a mirror and every handle on the cabinets had been wiped down at least four times.

Every dish in each cabinet had been washed and put back carefully in perfect order after she had wiped down the insides of each cabinet.

The modern steel appliances didn't have a fingerprint on them and a person could eat out of the sink it was so clean.

The kitchen smelled like a combination of lemon juice and bleach. She had a hunch the smell was far stronger than she was noticing, considering how many hours she had been using the cleaner.

She eased her shoulders up and down a few times to loosen them and took another sip of her almost-cold coffee. She had made the coffee after her shower, then had spent too long in the bathroom working on her brown hair trying to get it perfect. But after three hours of intense cleaning, she had to get herself clean as well.

And perfect.

Everything had to be perfect.

And now, finally, it was.

She turned slowly in the kitchen, studying to see if she had missed any detail at all. She had even climbed up and cleaned off the top of the refrigerator. Any blood drops would be easy to find now.

She let out a deep sigh that seemed to echo in the large, suburban home. She had so loved this house when she and Dead Man had bought it. They had been so happy.

Three bedrooms that they talked about using for future children, a two-car garage where her Mercedes lived beside his Lexus, and a kitchen she always described to friends as perfect.

They had even had the back lawn that looked out over the city below refurbished and put in two swings. She had spent many a summer's night sitting in that swing staring out at the city.

She had someday hoped her children would use the swings. Now that would never happen.

And last night, she had once again sat in the swing after she discovered his affair.

She had actually walked in on Dead Man and his secretary having sex on his desk in his office after hours. His desk stuff and some papers had scattered everywhere on the floor, making an awful mess, and Dead Man and his secretary had both been so preoccupied, they didn't notice Lacey peeking in and then filming them for a minute with her phone.

The secretary had blonde hair, much larger breasts than Lacey, and a slight roll of fat around her stomach. How could Dead Man even be interested in such a woman when he had a perfect-bodied wife at home?

Lacey had no idea what had gone wrong with Dead Man's thinking.

She and Dead Man were both thirty, both successful in real estate, both in love with each other.

Clearly not enough.

The sex had slowly faded to nothing over the last two years, even though she was going to the gym every day to keep fit and trim just for him.

Yesterday, she knew that their ideal marriage in their perfect home was over. Dead Man was sleeping with his secretary and there was no returning to marriage bliss from that.

In fact, in short order, there would be no more marriage. Period.

Perfect had been ruined for good for her.

She knew she could never live without perfect in her life. Perfect had become everything she lived for, actually.

And there was no point in continuing to live without perfect.

She took the half-cup of cold coffee and went down the tiled hall and into their master bedroom. The bed was made exactly, everything in its exact place on the dresser and vanity. She had laid out on the bed the perfect dress for the evening, something with some lace and trim and a nice pattern. Not a going-out-to-dinner dress, but not her exercise clothes either.

When she bought it, Dead Man had said it made her look younger and sexier.

She put it on, not bothering with underwear. The dress would be ruined anyway, so there was no point in also destroying perfectly fine underwear as well.

She then took her coffee cup, still half-full, and went back into their living room. On the inlaid mahogany coffee table in front of the big screen television, she had set up her phone to play Dead Man's sex scene with his secretary over and over again.

Luckily she hadn't recorded the sound of the sex. She would never want to hear that again.

She put her coffee cup on the table beside her phone, adjusting it so it looked like she had placed it there naturally. Then she did the unthinkable just a day ago.

She tipped it over, letting the coffee run away from her phone and off the coffee table and onto the tile floor.

At first she wanted to jump up and grab a cloth and clean up the mess. Then she realized that the mess was exactly what she wanted, what she had planned, and she forced herself to calm down.

Perfect.

She had made a perfect mess.

She glanced at the time on the big decorative wall clock over the kitchen.

Any moment now. Dead Man was always punctual coming home at exactly the time he said he would.

And right on time, the sound of the garage door opening rumbled faintly through the house.

She tapped the phone without shutting off the video. She had set the phone to send the film on the screen to Dead Man's boss and his secretary's husband and the police.

The message with the video to the police said simply, "He's going to kill me. I discovered his affair. Hurry."

And then she had typed in most of the Bryant Street

address, but cut off the last few letters to make it seem she had been interrupted. They would find the house easily.

She sat back on the couch, staring ahead at the screen as if she was in shock. She might have been in shock when she saw the scene in his office the first time, but now it just looked disgusting and messy and actually kind of boring.

And she could actually look at it now without seeing large clawed monsters crawling on both of them.

"Lacey," Dead Man said, the way he always did when he came home and her car was in the garage, "I'm home."

That had been funny for the first few months. After that it had just grown tiring.

She could hear him come into the living room behind her and then stop.

"Did you clean up your office or did you make her?" Lacey asked.

Dead Man said nothing.

Lacey could feel the thick tension in the air and she kind of liked that. It made her feel alive for the first time in a very long time. Too bad she was about to die.

In the distance she could hear the faint sounds of sirens, more than likely the police coming.

She stood and without looking at Dead Man, walked into her perfectly cleaned kitchen.

She took a long, very sharp carving knife from the knife block on the counter, then turned and said to him, "Might as well cut my heart out."

"Wouldn't that make a mess?" he asked, turning and moving toward her.

"Yeah, it would."

"You hate messes."

"I hate you more," she said, her voice calm even though she was having trouble breathing.

"Did you get off standing in the door watching me and Darla?" Dead Man asked. "Or were we covered in monsters?"

She wanted to take the knife and stab him at that moment. It had been slightly exciting, but she would never admit that to him.

She handed him the knife. "Go ahead, make a mess."

He did exactly as she knew he would do. He took the knife by the handle and then tossed it on the counter. He didn't put it back where it belonged, he didn't put it beside the sink to be cleaned later. He just tossed it aside.

What had she ever seen in this man?

"Being a little dramatic here, aren't you?" Dead Man asked.

She smiled as the sirens outside got louder. "You ruined my life."

"I think you did that all on your own," Dead Man said, shaking his head and looking sad. "When you had that affair with the broker and brought home crabs."

She shuddered. She had forgotten that.

She had never felt clean again after that.

Everything had changed.

Every time she and Dead Man had tried to make love after that, she imagined giant creatures swarming all over him. Twice she had thrown up on him.

And professional help had done no good.

In fact, it was the professionals who suggested that to get past the mistake she had made and the problems she had caused and the images of giant crab-like monsters on people and herself, she needed to keep clean.

Now she kept everything clean.

"So you called the police again?" Dead Man said, shaking his head and looking at her.

She could no longer tell what his expressions meant.

"Again?" she asked, feeling confused.

Dead Man pointed to the screen in the living room replaying his affair. "Lacey, you know, if you let yourself remember, that's not me. That's an old clip you found on the Internet five months ago. You just believe it's me and my secretary to make yourself feel better."

She glanced at the screen of the man going at the woman on the desk. Of course that was Dead Man. She had watched him, she had caught him, she had filmed him.

"You want me to have an affair so that everything is even. You said that once. But I only love you. Only you."

Her perfect plan was falling apart.

"As the doctors told you," Dead Man said, "you are just trying to blame me for your affair."

"You ruined our perfect life," she said, trying to keep her voice level, but she knew she couldn't hold on much more.

"I have never had an affair," he said. "You had the affair and ruined our perfect life. You are the one that can't seem to let go of the fact that you caught crabs and let us move on together. I have forgiven you from day one. Remember? You need to forgive yourself."

She shook her head violently from side-to-side.

"That's not true!"

"Of course it's true, Lacey," Dead Man said.

Behind them the police knocked and then came in. One was a young man looking puzzled and the other was an older guy by the name of Donny. She knew him from somewhere.

"Lacey having troubles again?" Donny asked, looking genuinely concerned as he came up and stood beside Dead Man.

"More than likely forgot to take her meds again," Dead Man said.

"The place does smell of cleaning solution," Donny said, nodding.

Lacey couldn't believe all this was happening. They were talking about her as if she wasn't there. Her perfect plan was ruined. They had got to her before she could stab herself and make it look like Dead Man did it.

"I'm sorry, Devin," Donny said. "What can we do?"

"Just leave me alone!" Lacey shouted.

She bolted for the back door and out into the yard. There she climbed into the swing that looked out over the beautiful lights of the city. The stars were out and there was a full moon.

She made herself take a few deep breaths and gaze out over the perfect view.

This was perfect.

Absolutely perfect.

From the porch she heard Donny say, "We have an ambulance on the way."

"Thanks," Dead Man said. "That will be perfect."

Both he and Donny chuckled slightly, but Lacey thought they were right.

Perfect.

Smith's STORIES

Dean Wesley Smith

A Brush with Intent
A Bryant Street Story

BRYANT STREET

A BRUSH WITH INTENT

On Bryant Street, really strange things happen. Usually they exist with a fantasy twist or a Twilight Zone feel.

But every-so-often other things happen. Normal things.

Things that real-world people deal with in a place, in a neighborhood, they really love.

JD Steinhauer sat at his wooden dining room table, classic rock songs from his distant youth playing softly on the radio. Around him the familiar kitchen with drawings from the grandkids on the fridge, the tan blinds over the windows, and the photos of family and old friends, many now gone, filling the wall behind him.

Em, his wonderful and still beautiful wife of fifty-seven years, sat in her chair in the living room facing the television. It was on, but the sound was turned down. Em didn't care.

Her gray hair was pulled back and tied like she liked it, her blouse today was blue to go along with blue slacks and her blue slippers. She had always liked to dress in similar colors each day.

But now Em didn't much care about anything and he dressed her each morning since her mind had slowly vanished. She no longer recognized him or their two kids or the three grandkids.

Luckily, if there was such a thing in these circumstances, she could be easily directed and never really complained. So every morning he walked her carefully through her morning routine, keeping it exactly the same as she used to do when she did it herself.

He helped her get dressed, always asking her opinion on one bit of clothing or another, even though she never responded. He helped her eat, then he took her to her chair and turned on the television.

Except for occasional bathroom breaks and lunch and dinner, that was how she spent her days.

And he spent his days hovering nearby, making sure she was all right and getting her anything she needed. He never left the house anymore and did nothing at all for himself. He didn't really mind. They knew that going into old age would be rough if they survived. And they both had.

Sort of.

He just hated to see her end up this way.

She had always had a vibrant way about her, a smile

that lit up any room, and an energy that never seemed to stop. For decades she would often get up ahead of him and stay up long after he went to bed.

She had worked as a teacher for forty years, seeming to love every minute of it. She volunteered in local charities, and raised their kids, all without a complaint. She had been, and she still was an amazing woman.

He always wondered how he had gotten so lucky to have her love him.

Now he would take care of her until his old body wouldn't let him anymore. Then they would move together into a nice place he and Danny, his son, had found. There JD could get help with Em.

They had the place reserved and waiting for JD to call Danny and they would just move. It could be done on an hour's notice. Danny had already taken over clothes and bathroom items for both of them.

JD was afraid that today might be that time. He had let Em slip in the shower this morning, but caught her before she fell, wrenching his own back in the process.

That was only a dull throb now, but he had a hunch tomorrow morning would be a problem for him. His back had never been that good to start with and when he wrenched it, he often couldn't get out of bed in the morning.

He looked around the small dining area and then into the living room at Em. They would eventually need to sell their home here on Bryant Street to afford the small apartment they were moving into in the full-care facility. But not right away. Maybe in a year or two.

Assuming they both lived that long. If not, Danny would sell it. It was going to him and his sister anyway.

Em was sitting, staring at the television. She seldom moved, her perfect profile still holding her back straight and her chin up.

He stood, his back twitching from the new injury, and moved over to her.

"Sweetie, I think it's time we go to our new place."

He had told her many times about how good it was. He doubted she had heard him.

He touched her shoulder, knowing she really didn't understand him this time either.

But to his surprise, she turned and looked up at him and for a moment the old Em was in her deep brown eyes. "Do what you need to do for us," she said. "You know I hate being this way and not being able to help."

"I know," he said, kneeling down beside her so he could look directly into her eyes.

"I'm not going to get any better," she said. "I love this house, but I am not going to get any better. Do what you need to do for both of us."

"I know that as well. And I will. I will always love you and be beside you."

She nodded slightly and then the light and life seemed to just drain away from her eyes and she turned back to stare at the silent television.

That was the first episode in weeks where she had been in her mind. He treasured every one of them.

He made sure she was comfortable, then moved slowly back over to the table and eased his old, aching body into a chair.

She really had loved this home, even more than he had. He loved the neighborhood, the ease of moving around, and how much love the two of them had shared in these walls over the three-plus decades here.

They had raised their kids here.

All the good times with Em had been in this house.

He looked over at her and smiled.

Maybe he could make it another day here.

Just one more day.

Smith's STORIES

DEAN WESLEY SMITH

A HOME FOR THE BOOKS

A Bryant Street Story

BRYANT STREET

A HOME FOR THE BOOKS

Gerald Earnst loves old books. He loves the smell of them, the feel of the leather, the smoothness of the dust jackets.

He and his wife Bettie met in a bookstore, bonded over old books, and filled their house on Bryant Street with wonderful books.

Then after Bettie died, Gerald didn't stop as only someone living on Bryant Street could do.

———

Gerald Earnst loved old books. He loved their smell. The feel of old leather covers. The slickness of dust jackets. He even didn't mind paperbacks, both the trade and mass-market size.

He just loved books. Period.

His few friends called him pathological about books. He knew he was. He didn't care.

Ten years ago, he and his wonderful wife, Bettie, had bought a house on Bryant Street. A simple, three bedroom with two baths. They both loved books and had actually met in a bookstore in the mystery section.

She worked in a local bank as an assistant manager and he worked as an architect in an office just four blocks away from Bettie. Every day they met for lunch, usually just soup or sandwiches, then spent the last half of their lunchtime in one of three local bookstores, searching for that next treasure.

At home she used one bedroom as a sewing room, he used the other one for his habit of buying books online, and sometimes even selling a few when he had duplicates.

That made getting the packages every day and opening them exciting for both of them.

Every room of their house had books in it. The living and dining rooms had beautiful custom-made, floor-to-ceiling oak bookshelves and Gerald and Betty put their most expensive collectable books on those. The rest of the rooms had pine shelves that worked great and when Bettie died of cancer, they had pretty much filled up every wall of every room with every type of book.

The entire house was a shrine to their thirty years of marriage in books.

Gerald missed Bettie more than he wanted to admit, so he decided he wouldn't move a book from its position on the shelves on the day she died.

But he still wanted to buy more books, and he did, knowing that some of them Bettie would have loved. But they started stacking up in boxes since he had nowhere to put them until one day, at work, he noticed he was working on the plans of a house with a basement.

It would be possible to dig a basement under his Bryant Street home to get more room for his books.

As it had happened, a month after Bettie died, an uncle of his died and Gerald ended up the major heir and got more money than he would know what to do with.

So he got the plans worked out, got all the permits, and hired the crew to build a basement under his home. And this basement also went out under the backyard, so not only did he double the square footage of his home, he almost tripled it.

And he designed all the rooms in the basement for the best use of walls for shelves and had the contractors just build all the shelves as they went. Floor-to-ceiling shelves in every room and hallway.

And some rooms had shelves in the middle of the rooms, making those rooms look like a library.

He added in a small office with a bed and a bathroom, plus a small kitchen as well so he never had to go upstairs just for food or to sleep.

It took the crews almost six months to build the basement. They hauled all the dirt out the back and out the alley behind the house. From the front of the house, you could never tell major construction was happening.

By that time most of his garage was filled with boxes of books he had bought.

He kept buying as he put the books he had already bought on shelves.

Bettie would have loved the basement addition. He wished she was there to see it.

One year later, Gerald realized he was going to have a problem. His new basement was almost half full.

He was going to run out of room again.

So one week later, Gerald went back to talk with the contractor who had done the work on his basement to ask him if he could go another level deeper. In other words, put a basement under the basement.

Gerald had done all the plans for the next level down, and knew it was possible, but he also knew that it would never be permitted. The second basement would have to be done without permits.

The contractor at first just said no.

Gerald showed him the plans.

Contractor said it would never get a permit.

Gerald showed him a check for ten times the amount the contractor had got for the first basement, and then said, "This is the down. You get equal amount when finished."

Contractor agreed and they worked out how the work would be done, in the day, with a permit to work on the basement they had finished the previous year, put in a new bath. So the job site would have a permit, just not for the job being done.

Four months later, Gerald had a sub-basement, just as big as the basement above, with massive floor-to-ceiling bookshelves forming nothing but aisles between the support pillars holding up the basement and house above it. They didn't even pretend to put in rooms this time. Just pillars and bookshelves.

Gerald figured the new basement would hold twice the number of books that the basement and the entire house above it held.

And he had even put in a hidden door from the first basement down into his new basement.

Empty shelves. And he had more than enough money to buy books.

If Bettie had been here, this would be heaven.

So for the next four years, he did that. Worked at his job during the day and bought books the rest of the time.

Wonderful old books that smelled of leather and felt heavy in his hand.

And he spent hours and hours every day moving books from one place to another to try to keep them in order by genre and then by author name. It tired him out, but he loved it.

And he had learned to always unpack the new books coming into the house in the kitchen upstairs and put the books in cloth bags with handles so he could carry them down the stairs.

He never touched the books on the main floor of the house. He left them how they had been when Bettie died.

And every night, when he got exhausted from carrying books downstairs and moving them around, he would take one book and go upstairs to his chair in the living room and read.

Finally, at sixty-six years of age, Gerald retired and could spend every minute of every day buying books and trying to put them in order. But he just didn't have the energy he used to have, so the boxes of books he found online started to pile up once again in the garage. He just couldn't unpack them fast enough and get them down to the basement or the sub-basement and on shelves fast enough.

And then one day, at the age of seventy, he had a heart attack while unpacking a box of books on his kitchen table. He managed to call for help and ended up getting a bypass and spending weeks away from his books and then weeks more recovering at home, with a nursing service bringing him food and helping him with recovery.

He did not see his basement or his sub-basement in that entire time. And he realized that if he died, all of his and Bettie's wonderful books would be lost.

So for the next few weeks as he recovered, instead of buying more books, he emailed and phoned bookstores within a hundred-mile radius, basically looking for a young person who was passionate about buying books.

And that was when he realized that the world had really, really changed. There were many, many younger people who loved books and reading, but they did it all online. And read books on their phones.

No one he could find under fifty was passionate about collecting the old books and reading a book while holding it in his hand.

He was old and sick and alone and he had hundreds and hundreds of thousands of old books in his home on a regular subdivision street and when he died, no one would care.

He talked with libraries over the next few days, but not one library would even consider that size of donation. Not a one of them could begin to handle it.

One person at one library even laughed and said, "You could have a garage sale."

So that night, Gerald sat in his comfortable reading chair, his feet up, slippers off, but his reading book was beside him, and he was just staring at the walls of books around him.

He just sat there thinking and looking at all the walls of books in sight of his chair.

One book clearly in his sight was one of Bettie's favorite books. And a couple over was another of her favorite books. She had treasured both of them and both of them brought back memories every time she touched the book.

"What am I going to do, Bettie?" he asked. "I want the books you and I have found to be appreciated."

Then, as if Bettie told him what to do, he had a plan.

The next day he talked to three of his favorite bookstore employees at local bookstores and asked them if they would like a second job that paid not only a lot of money per hour, but in special books. Evenings, mornings, weekends were fine.

All three were men in their thirties, clearly book people. They all knew each other. All of them were married, all had young kids, and all could use the extra money.

Gerald told them that the job was working with books.

They all agreed.

So together the next afternoon, all three of them got a tour of the house and both basements and all three were completely shocked at what he had done.

One of them had to help him back up the stairs to the main part of the house.

After he sat down at his kitchen table and had them take seats around the table, he said, "Now you see the problem. My wife and I would love to have these books go to people who would still appreciate classic paper books. But as a collection, it is far too large, and as you can see, I can no longer go up and down those stairs to enjoy my passion of working with books."

All three nodded.

"So with all of your help," he said, "instead of me buying books, I'm going to give them away, each book to someone who would really wants that certain book."

"Give them away?" all three asked at once.

Gerald just nodded. And told them his plan.

Gerald wanted the three of them to offer one book per person, free. He wanted the offer to go out on book sites, on media sites, anyplace they could think of putting this out.

Even posters in the bookstores they worked at if their bosses would allow it.

All the person who wanted the book had to do was tell Gerald in an essay why they wanted the book and why it was important to them.

"Any book?"

"Any book," Gerald said. "And we ship it for free. They get the book in the mail without cost if I believe their reason for wanting it is valid."

All three looked stunned.

It was at that moment Gerald started just calling them "The Three."

"And if I don't have the book they want here in these three levels," Gerald said, "we'll go in search of it and buy it, within reason, and send it to that person, again if we believe their reason is valid."

Gerald went on. "But let's have everyone give us an alternative to two."

So all three agreed they wanted the job.

Gerald had them buy three new computers to put on his dining room table, and the word started to spread.

A month later, three times a day Gerald sat with a stack of paper with essays on them, reading about why a person thought a book important in their lives.

He could tell the real ones from the "just want a free expensive book" ones. And his three employees were shipping out books at a steady stream.

The only moment Gerald had trouble with the plan was

when someone requested one of Bettie's favorite books. But that trouble was only for a moment, and he let it go.

And then slowly, over a year's time, the requests slowed to a few a day, more than likely since they had limited one free book per person.

So Gerald called a meeting of The Three. He had really come to admire and like all of them and watched how well they worked together. They had even invited him to a barbeque where all three of their families got together. But more than anything, he loved their passion about books.

"My doctor tells me that my time is short," Gerald said. "And it looks like our program has given a lot of joy to a lot of people around the world, but is winding down."

The three all agree that it had.

"But we have a lot of books left. Still far, far too many to deal with."

Again they all agreed.

"So if you three think you can work together," Gerald said, "I'm going to fund a bookstore up completely with large reserve funds and make all three of you equal owners and move all of these books into the store."

Gerald stared at three shocked faces.

"If you decide you want to do this, the corporation that owns the store that all three of you will own equal parts in, will pay you all a good living wage."

Gerald gave them the address of a massive empty store that had anchored one of the malls in town. It would be on the first day it opened one of the largest bookstores in ten states.

"Go take a look at that, see what you think of a bookstore in there with the focus on bringing back people reading hardback and paper books. Then come back tomorrow. I will have contracts for you to sign and a way to work together so you won't kill each other."

He made them leave without asking any more questions, then he just sat in his chair and smiled.

"Bettie," he said. "I think I found a home for all of our wonderful books."

The next day all three agreed and they signed the papers and Gerald transferred over a million dollars into the new corporation account his attorney had set up for the store.

And officially, in the papers, he had sold all the books. Plus he had sold the bookstore company the house on Bryant Street to them as well, for them to do with as they pleased after he died or was moved out.

And he paid for his contractor who had done the work on his basements to build beautiful shelves as the three wanted and Gerald even dug out a sketch pad and helped them with the design of the overall store.

He was surprised and pleased that in something like that they didn't even argue much.

In four months, the shelves were done, the front area was built, the offices were done. All three of the owners had agreed that a major online presence to buy and sell books was critical, so a large computer area was built as well just for that.

And Gerald asked them if he could buy books online

and donate them to the store and they all laughed and said, "of course."

Then, on the anniversary of Bettie's death, they started packing and moving books to the store.

Gerald just sat and watched as they brought box after box up the stairs.

They started in the sub-basement and it took thirty-one large U-Haul trucks over two weeks to get those books moved and on shelves in the new store.

Every day they brought him pictures of the books slowly filling the store shelves. It was wonderful to see.

Then the next week they packed and moved all the books in the regular basement, this time it took only twenty large trucks.

They also got all the boxes of books out of the garage, the ones he had never had a chance to even open or hold the books in them.

He hadn't decided which of the books he wanted moved out of the main floor. For sure the ones in Bettie's sewing room and his old office. But the ones in the hallway and in the dining and living room and his bedroom he kind of wanted to leave for now on the walls.

He just couldn't imagine living in a world that didn't have books covering the walls.

He would tell them that when they arrived for the first truckload in the morning.

It didn't matter.

He died in his sleep that night and they found him the next morning, a book he had been reading on his chest.

His entire estate went to the bookstore with the sole purpose of buying and selling paper books and keeping his and Bettie's love for them alive.

And the house on Bryant Street was sold six months later to two young booklovers whose collection almost filled all the shelves on the main floor when they moved in.

But they were young and they had time and a lot of room to expand.

Smith's STORIES

Dean Wesley Smith
Kill for a Statistic
A Bryant Street Story

BRYANT STREET

KILL FOR A STATISTIC

Damon Felt, a walking, talking cliché of a meek human, lived on Bryant Street. Pathetically normal to fifty levels, Damon Felt did not belong on Bryant Street.

Carson Range, a self-appointed expert on the strangeness that existed on Bryant Street knew it without a doubt. But yet Damon Felt lived there, normal as anyone.

Until one day Damon showed his true colors. And Carson needed to walk away. Maybe run.

Damon Felt worked in a bank, for heaven's sake. He wore bottle-sized glasses and a wool suit that seemed slightly too large for his tiny frame, and when he moved he seemed deathly afraid of bumping into anyone or even being noticed.

He was a walking, talking cliché of a meek human, more than likely too afraid to stand up and say anything at all, which chances are had kept him in his assistant to an assistant manager position for ten years. His actual title was Vault and New Accounts Manager.

Seriously, who made up this stuff?

Everything I had seen and found out about him painted him as exactly what he seemed in real life. A 125-pound man who just got by in life. His meager salary paid his expenses and utilities for his nondescript suburban home on Bryant Street to the south of Las Vegas in Henderson, and left him enough for food, television cable, and a nice meal out at a local restaurant every Thursday night promptly at six.

Of all the twisted psychos and subdivision nutjobs I had investigated on Bryant Street, Damon Felt was the most puzzling. Pathetically normal to fifty levels. I just knew there had to be something deep inside him that drove him to buy a house on Bryant Street.

No one just accidently bought a home on Bryant Street in any subdivision in any city. I know.

My name is Carson Range and I have been stalking the secret of this stupid street for a decade now. And without a doubt, because of my obsession with the street, I was going to be dead a lot sooner than I would have expected.

Bryant Street was that kind of place.

My entire journey to my death started with an assignment by an editor at a paper I used to work for in Oregon about a number of weird events on the same subdivision street. And the more I dug, the more I realized that the street was just a wasteland of screwed-up humans.

And it seemed that everyone who buys a home on the street is drawn to the street for a reason. And it's not some magic thing, I am sure, but a force that makes people think the standard suburban street is special.

Well, Bryant Street is special, just not in the way they all first think.

When I changed jobs to a paper in Denver, I learned that the Bryant Street there had just a screwed-up history as the one outside of Portland, Oregon.

By my best count, doing a ton of research, which as a reporter I am damn good at, there are over 400 miles of Bryant Streets in the suburbs of twelve major cities. Some of the streets are only a block or so long, a couple streets go on for miles.

Every last one of them has registered a number of strange events, deaths, murders, missing persons, and so on.

The newest Bryant Street appeared in a new subdivision of Las Vegas in the Henderson area in 2005. That one scared me because it actually wound through the hills for just under three miles.

That is a lot of screwed up, let me tell you.

And promises of even more screwed-up messes.

I moved to Vegas in 2010 and got myself a good deal on a small home in North Las Vegas, just about as far across the Vegas Valley as I could get from Bryant Street. I didn't need anything more than a small house since I was single at the age of thirty-eight and planned to remain that way.

Damon Felt, meek banker and cliché, had bought a home on Bryant Street during the worst of the Las Vegas real estate recession of 2008. For what it is worth now in 2022, he made a killing.

Since I started to work for a local Vegas paper and kept an eye on Bryant Street, there had been a dozen deaths in eleven years on the street, seven people were hospitalized with mental health issues, four people went missing, and two of the houses burnt to the ground.

Five more houses along the three miles are sitting empty and in some sort of limbo because of missing owners, even in the hot real estate market.

I now have files on eighty people or couples or families who live on the street, and all of them had one issue or another.

Except for Damon Felt.

I had to try to figure out what drove him to live on that street.

So I did what any busy person would do when faced with a need and a little too much money. I set up surveillance cameras watching his home. Cost me a pretty penny, but was worth it.

I even managed to get one hidden on a garage behind his house.

The cameras were motion activated and I downloaded the server and reset everything remotely every two days.

Holy shit was Damon Felt boring.

In the months I watched him and his stupid schedule, one house on Bryant Street burned down and two of the other residents died in one fashion or another.

But good old Damon Felt did exactly the same thing every day, left for work and came home at exactly the same time, turned off his bedroom light at exactly the same time.

Day after day, month after month, always the same.

Right up until the point that it wasn't.

I had hired a computer hacker to dig into Damon Felt's finances and he got me one detail I didn't know about. Damon had a storage unit about four blocks from his home.

And I had a private detective teach me how to track Damon's new minivan. Always a gray one that he traded in every year for a new one that looked identical. He always paid cash. It seemed the newer the car, the easier it was to track. Who knew?

So I got all that set up, and waited for more months.

Boring months.

Damon Felt always kept to his exact schedule. He never went to his storage unit.

Until he did.

And every day after that first day, his storage unit became part of Damon Felt's schedule.

He didn't seem to be moving anything in the van, but he went there every day and stayed exactly thirty minutes and then went home.

Now, to say at this time that I was obsessed with Bryant Street and Damon Felt would be a very sad understatement.

Thankfully I was single, didn't drink much, loved my

reporting job, and had enough money to live nice. I didn't much care for any form of gambling, considering my reporting job enough of a gamble.

But Bryant Street and Damon Felt had me hooked, like a smoker just wanting one more cigarette before promising to quit.

Well, my one more cigarette would kill me. I just didn't know it.

So when I realized Damon's routine had altered so that he spent time in his storage unit every day, I rented one right across the narrow, paved road from his.

I got a bunch of empty boxes from a stationary store and wrote on them in big black felt marker so they looked like there was something in them. Then I took my bike that I hadn't used in years and some other stuff and after three trips across town, I had the small unit looking like I was actually storing stuff in it.

Then parking my car away from my storage unit because I didn't want Damon recognizing it, I had the door open to my unit when he arrived.

It was a moderately warm spring afternoon, sunny as always, with almost no wind. I pretended to work arranging the boxes.

Damon arrived looking exactly like he looked in the bank. Wool suit, bland tie, thinning hair combed perfectly.

He got out of his van, locked it, and then unlocked his storage unit.

As the door went up, I could see he had hung a privacy curtain about two feet deep inside.

What the hell was that for? What was he doing in there?

He looked around, but I had timed that moment to have my back turned so he wouldn't think I was paying attention, then he pulled the curtain aside and ducked in, letting the curtain fall back into place.

But what I saw in that unit turned my blood cold.

For a second I thought what I saw was women's bodies.

You know, active imagination.

I took a breath and realized what I had seen were mannequins.

Naked women's mannequins.

And they had been smashed up something awful, at least the ones I caught a glimpse of.

Then, from the other side of the curtain I heard a shout.

"Take that!"

And there was a smash that echoed along the narrow road between rows of storage units.

Then a moment later another, "Take that!"

Followed by another smash.

I ran across the short distance to his storage unit, stopped just short of the curtain, and said, "You all right in there? I heard a crash."

"I am fine," Damon Felt said. "Please come in. But watch your step."

I pulled back the curtain and stepped inside.

The storage unit was a large one, a good twenty feet deep and twenty feet wide. Five or six bulbs hung from cords giving the place a very bright feel.

And it was full of female mannequins in different states

of wholeness. Numbers of them had the empty painted eyes staring up at me from a head on the ground. There had to be a good fifty of them, the ones to the back less damaged. He clearly had been beating on the ones at the front.

"This is quite satisfying," Damon Felt said, actually smiling. "Would you like to try?"

He offered the bat in his hand to me.

I think I actually shuddered.

Not once in my life, with all my dates, girlfriends, and two fiancées, had I ever been angry enough at a woman to take a bat to her.

Not once, not even close.

Never crossed my mind, to be honest.

The entire scene just sickened me.

"My online therapist tells me this would be good for my pent-up aggressions."

I nodded, and Damon Felt looked at the different pieces of mannequins and smiled. "Surprisingly, it really does help."

Again I just nodded.

This guy was one sick human.

Damon smiled again, holding the aluminum bat. "After a few more days I might take some pieces of these home and see if I can build a brand new woman. That should be entertaining."

At that moment I knew that Damon Felt belonged completely on Bryant Street.

"It would be a lot more fun than spying on someone you don't know," he said. "Don't you think, Mr. Range?"

What he said took me a second to register that he knew what I had been doing. But by that point it was too late.

My obsession had caught up with me like that one last cigarette.

The bat caught me against the side of my head and sent me stumbling into the aluminum wall and down to the ground.

God that hurt.

I tried to climb back to my feet, but nothing seemed to want to work.

"Putting together mannequin parts should be a lot easier than real women," Damon Felt said. "I have tried that and I never seem to make it work."

I struggled to climb to my feet, but without luck. Why didn't I just trust that he lived on Bryant Street for a reason and leave it alone?

Too late now.

Damon Felt smiled. "Don't worry, I won't use any of your parts. I don't really like men."

The last thing I saw was Damon Felt's small smiling face an instant before the bat sent me spinning down into darkness to become just another statistic of Bryant Street.

USA *Today* Bestselling Writer

DEAN WESLEY SMITH

To Remember A Single Minute

BRYANT STREET

TO REMEMBER A SINGLE MINUTE

Remember Incorporated. A company that promises that once the disease took Mike Hanley's mind, he would remember one single minute of his life in stark clarity.

Any minute.

He just needs to pick the minute.

But of all the wonderful minutes in his entire life, which one can he pick?

A Bryant Street story with a haunting question.

ONE

Mike Hanley stared at the sign over the large double glass doors tucked into the impressive gray stone building.

Remember Incorporated

People were coming and going through the doors under the sign like any normal business office.

He stood across the street, his back against the wall of another building, just watching, trying to keep his old and frail body from being trampled by office workers in a hurry to get somewhere.

When he was younger, he had always been in a hurry as well. He couldn't remember where exactly he was in a hurry to go on any given day, but he remembered the sensation of always being in that state of mind.

The day around him was warm, not hot, just warm, and the sidewalks on both sides of the busy four-lane street were crowded with all types, almost all wearing in one form or another the traditional New York black.

He loved this city. He had lived here his entire life.

That morning in his little retirement apartment bedroom, he had combed what was left of his gray hair, had donned a brown Ben Hogan-style golf hat, a new pair of blue slacks, and a loud orange shirt with dark blue suspenders. He knew he looked more like a clown than an eighty-nine-year-old man, but he didn't care and it would make no difference.

He would never remember today.

The instructions that *Remember Incorporated* had given him were clear. He needed to pick one minute of his life to remember before he walked through the door.

And the memory had to be a clear one, sharp, usable.

TO REMEMBER A SINGLE MINUTE

One minute. Only one minute. That was so unfair.

As an architect and avid outdoors person, he had lived a full life, teeming with millions of minutes he wanted to remember and standing there on the sidewalk, he could remember every one of them like they were yesterday.

He and Carol had had a wonderful fifty-five years together, raising three fantastic kids that he loved more than anything. All of that time was full of minutes worth remembering as well.

He stood for a moment, smiling, remembering all the good times.

Of course, along the way there were a lot of minutes he didn't want to remember as well, including the minute Carol died last fall. Nothing had been the same since, and when he got the diagnosis that he would be losing his memories fairly quickly over the next few months, he wanted to try to save something of his life.

Remember Incorporated had told him that they could save one minute of his memories for him.

A minute he could always remember. Even when his disease took him down.

A minute would be better than nothing.

Remember Incorporated did it for free. No cost, just a service they provided for seniors such as himself. So no scam, no tricks, nothing.

They offered him one minute.

But from a full, rich life with a million memories all flooding at him as he stood there on the sidewalk, which minute could he pick?

Maybe it was just better to let them all go.

TWO

Mike Hanley stared at the sign over the large double glass doors tucked into the impressive gray stone building.

Remember Incorporated

People were coming and going through the doors under the sign like any normal business office.

He stood across the street, his back against the wall of another building, just watching, trying to keep his old and frail body from being trampled by office workers in a hurry to get somewhere.

When he was younger, he had always been in a hurry as well. He couldn't remember where exactly he was in a hurry to go on any given day, but he remembered the sensation of always being in that state of mind.

The day around him was warm, not hot, just warm, and the sidewalks on both sides of the busy four-lane street were crowded with all types, almost all wearing in one form or another the traditional New York black.

He loved this city. He had lived here his entire life.

That morning in his little retirement apartment bedroom, he had combed what was left of his gray hair, had donned a brown Ben Hogan-style golf hat, a new pair of blue slacks, and a loud orange shirt with dark blue suspenders. He knew he looked more like a clown than an eighty-nine-year-old man, but he didn't care and it would make no difference.

He would never remember today.

The instructions that *Remember Incorporated* had given him were clear. He needed to pick one minute of his life to remember before he walked through the door.

"Dad?" the voice said, cutting through his memory.

The memory drifted into the background like smoke Mike couldn't seem to hold onto.

"Dad, are you awake?"

Mike Hanley glanced up at the face of a smiling man who had called him dad. He had no idea who the person was. Or even what a dad was, for that matter.

"I'm awake," Mike said.

"I brought you some lunch," the man said, sitting down beside him and helping him get hold of the thing with three points on it. The man helped Mike with what he called lunch, then wiped off his face and took the tray away.

Mike watched him go, not really remembering why the man had been there in the first place.

Everything was so puzzling to Mike. He felt at times that he should know something or someone, but just didn't.

He closed his eyes and a memory came flooding back in like smoke filling an empty balloon.

Mike was staring at the sign over the large double glass doors tucked into the impressive gray stone building.

Remember Incorporated

People were coming and going through the doors under the sign like any normal business office.

He stood across the street, his back against the wall of another building, just watching, trying to keep his old and frail body from being trampled by office workers in a hurry to get somewhere.

When he was younger, he had always been in a hurry as well. He couldn't remember where exactly he was in a hurry to go on any given day, but he remembered the sensation of always being in that state of mind.

The day around him was warm, not hot, just warm, and the sidewalks on both sides of the busy four-lane street were crowded with all types, almost all wearing in one form or another the traditional New York black.

He loved this city. He had lived here his entire life.

That morning in his little retirement apartment bedroom, he had combed what was left of his gray hair, had donned a brown Ben Hogan-style golf hat, a new pair of blue slacks, and a loud orange shirt with dark blue suspenders. He knew he looked more like a clown than an eighty-nine-year-old man, but he didn't care and it would make no difference.

He would never remember today.

The instructions that *Remember Incorporated* had given him were clear. He needed to pick one minute of his life to remember before he walked through the door.

And the memory had to be a clear one, sharp, usable.

One minute. Only one minute.

That was so unfair.

BRYANT STREET

Smith's
STORIES

Dean Wesley Smith
A Song For The Old Memory
A Bryant Street Story

BRYANT STREET

A SONG FOR THE OLD MEMORY

Ryan Peterson died on garbage day, alone in his home on Bryant Street. From there, nothing happens the way it should.
After all, he did live on Bryant Street.

Ryan Peterson died at just a little after eleven in the morning on a Tuesday.

Garbage day.

Ryan hated garbage day, even more so now that his wife of fifty-five years, Connie, was gone. He had managed once again to get the green trashcan on wheels down his short driveway to the edge of Bryant Street to be picked up.

Later in the evening, he would pull it back into position inside his double car garage. The only time these days he even bothered to open that garage door was for garbage day. He had given up driving and sold his car five years before.

He had closed the garage door, gone into his kitchen to get a glass of water, turned on the radio to his favorite oldies channel, and as the song "Crimson and Clover" started to play, he sat down at his kitchen table and just died, slumping forward like he was napping on the table, something Connie would have hated.

But Connie was no longer around. She hadn't been for years, and no one ever came to see him. Seems he could die where he damn well pleased.

He was eighty-nine, no kids, no real friends left alive. He had promised Connie before she died that he would take care of their home for as long as he could. Seems now he couldn't do that anymore.

He stood beside his kitchen counter, staring at his own dead body, feeling not really much of anything about being dead. At his age he had been expecting it for a very long time. He was just glad it hadn't been painful.

"Crimson and Clover" kept playing on his radio over and over as he stood there, as if the station had gotten a record stuck. The song had been annoying to him back when it was new, now after hearing it for a thousand times over the decades, he hated it.

And it wasn't going away even though he was dead.

He tried to reach over and turn off the radio, but of course his hand went through the radio.

Of course he was a ghost. Ghosts don't touch things. He knew that from all the television shows.

He glanced around, expecting to see some white light coming to get him.

Nope.

No white light, no Connie to greet him, nothing.

He wanted Connie to great him, to hug him, tell him everything would be all right.

But nothing.

Just the same home he had lived in alone now for seven long years and an annoying song going on and on.

He figured that maybe the white light was outside, so he headed for the front door of his three-bedroom ranch. He went to reach for the knob, but again his hand went through it.

"Going to take some getting used to," he said.

Then he tried to stick his hand through the wooden door, but it hit solid wood.

He pounded on the door and the walls, making no sounds at all, but not going through the walls either.

Starting to feel a little panicked, he went to the garage door and had the same luck. He couldn't open it, but he couldn't go through it either.

He went back in and stood beside his dead body. "Crimson and Clover" was playing over and over on the radio.

He made himself take a deep breath, then try to think. What would he have done if he hadn't died? He would have read the morning newspaper, which was folded on the kitchen table.

He tried to pick it up, but his hand passed through it.

He finally went to his recliner in the living room in front of the blank television screen, but he couldn't get the recliner to recline, or the television to come on, so he moved to the couch and just lay down, staring at the white ceiling, trying to ignore the words to "Crimson and Clover."

He must have dozed off because the next thing he knew the garbage truck was outside, making its normal banging and clanging sounds.

He stood and went to the window, carefully putting his face through the drapes and resting his nose on the hard glass surface so he could watch them. The day was sunny and bright and his lawn looked as green and fresh as he could remember it ever being. It wouldn't be in a week since he wouldn't be able to water it.

This week the garbage men actually managed to not spill any of his trash on the ground. They put the garbage can back where it belonged on the curb and moved on.

Ryan stared at the garbage can. It was going to sit there until someone found his body. He certainly never had to bring it back into the garage ever again.

But there was no telling how long it would be until someone found his body.

Maybe when they found him, he would be released from this house. He had always sort of felt it was a prison, but it had been Connie's dream home and he had lived his life for Connie.

And the last seven years since she died, he had just remained in her home, following the routines he had had with her. He shook his head at himself. He really had loved her more than he ever wanted to admit.

Now the house really was a prison. But he needed to make sure before he gave up.

He spent the next hour trying to go through walls and doors, pounding on windows until his fists hurt.

Nothing.

He was a ghost, stuck in a house with his own dead body, with the world's most annoying song playing over and over on the radio.

He went into the main bedroom, the one decorated by Connie all those years before, and stretched out on the bed. At least in here the song was fainter and he didn't have to look at his own body.

He went back to staring at the ceiling and again must have dozed.

He had nothing else to do.

He knew when a week had gone by because of the sound of the garbage men pulling up in front of his home and opening his garbage to see that it was empty. They shrugged and moved on.

The guy who mowed his lawn every other Monday came and went as well without noticing that the grass had started to turn brown.

And Ryan spent all of his time in his and Connie's bedroom down the hall because his body was starting to really smell and the song was still repeating on the radio.

Another week went past before the garbage men came again and this time they didn't just move on, but stopped and talked for a moment. By this point Ryan's grass had gone brown in the hot summer sun as well. Clearly there were signs something was wrong.

One of them came up and banged on the door a few times, then shook his head and went back to his coworker at the truck.

How in the world had they missed the smell of Ryan's rotting corpse?

Ryan cussed himself now for having his mail delivered to a PO Box and always buying his newspapers at the store down the street. Nothing but his lawn and the garbage can showed anyone that he was gone.

The second garbage man took the plastic container and pulled it up to the garage door and placed it there. Nice of him, but it screwed Ryan even more.

The following Monday the grass guy came back, cut the grass, knocked on the front door as well, and then shrugged and left.

Ryan retreated to the bedroom, lying on the bed and staring at the ceiling. "Connie," he said, after a moment, "I could use some help here if you can hear me."

Nothing changed.

He lay there, avoiding his own stench, waiting and dozing and thinking about his life. It had been a good life. Not exciting by any means, but perfect by his standards because he had met the woman of his dreams in college, got a good job, and that had been enough.

Connie had wanted this perfect (to her) home on Bryant Street and they had managed to buy it and pay it off in only twenty-five years. And on her deathbed she had made him promise to take care of the house and stay in it if he could.

He had promised.

He had just never expected the promise to go beyond death.

After another few weeks, the smell of his body seemed to be fading. He never looked at himself there slumped at the table. No point. He just mostly stayed on his side of the bed, staring at the ceiling, trying to remember the good times in his life.

Sadly, there were very few great times. Just lots and lots of normal times. Normal years.

Normal decades, actually.

More weeks went by.

His lawn had completely dried up, but a nice neighbor to his south started to water it and it was coming back to life now.

The first rain of the fall surprised Ryan. By his count he had been dead now for four months. And the song "Crimson and Clover" kept playing on his radio.

Finally, the power company cut off his power and the song ended.

And it wasn't until four or five days later of blessed silence in the house that he remembered that "Crimson and Clover" had been playing the moment he met Connie.

It hadn't been their song, but he remembered the moment in the Student Union at the university perfectly, how she had smiled at him, how he had felt shy and clumsy. And that song had been in the background.

Damn he missed her.

What had happened to her?

"About time you remembered that," Connie said, smiling at him as she took her normal spot on the right side of the bed beside him.

Ryan damned near rolled out of bed, he was so shocked.

She patted the blanket beside her and he moved over. He reached out and touched her hand and it felt warm and as he had remembered it seven years ago.

"Where have you been?" he asked.

She turned slightly and smiled at him. "I've been here the entire time."

"Since I died?" he asked.

"Since I died," she said. "I so love this house. Although it has a pretty nasty odor at the moment from your body."

"Not much I could have done about that," he said.

She squeezed his hand, accepting as she had always been.

"So when are we moving on from here?" he asked. "Into the light and all that?"

"I have no idea," she said. "I've been here the entire time since the moment I died. This is heaven to me, always will be. I don't want to move on and leave this wonderful place. Do you?"

He said nothing. Just held the hand of the woman of his dreams.

"Do you?" she asked again.

"I just want to be with you," he said. "That's all I've ever wanted in life."

She sighed that wonderful sigh he knew so well that meant she was contented. "You always say the most perfect things."

Side-by-side they lay there, weeks and months at a time, listening to the sounds of Bryant Street go on outside their perfect home.

They didn't talk much. After all the years, there was little left to talk about.

They just held hands, being together, and slowly fading away as the months and years went by.

And honestly, if Ryan had to think about it, that was a perfect way to go.

They were long gone when years later someone finally broke in to take over the house for unpaid back taxes and found Ryan's mummified remains still slumped over the kitchen table.

And when they turned the power back on, the first song that came over the radio was "Crimson and Clover."

Dean Wesley Smith

USA Today Bestselling Writer

CT#2

A perfect wife.
A perfect home.
A not-so-perfect husband.
What possibly
could go wrong?

Call Me Unfixable

A Bryant Street Story

BRYANT STREET

CALL ME UNFIXABLE

A perfect wife. A perfect home. A not-so-perfect husband.
What possibly could go wrong?
As a trial lawyer, Craig could face any situation and make it work. But facing his controlling wife and her lover (while they drank wine in his bed) turned out to need more than just a good plan.
Craig needed to believe in his actions, every action, no matter how small.
Or large.

Act One

I sat in my brand-new green Lexus on the hot pavement of Bryant Street and stared at the front door of my home across the lush and expensive green lawn, always perfectly kept, of course.

The car's engine idled almost silently and the air conditioning blew cold.

Before any rough day in court, as a major trial lawyer, I always sat in my car and made sure I was completely in character. The worst thing I could do in a courtroom was to have sudden doubts, or fall out of my belief system.

I thought of it as going on stage. I had to be completely in my character, completely submerged in the part I needed to play.

And that's what I had to do now. I had to stay in the part, in character. I couldn't let a stray thought break my concentration.

I again stared at the house. Right now the state-of-the-art sprinkler system was giving the lawn "just a taste" to keep it fresh looking even in the August heat. Most of the watering was done at night.

That stupid piece of green lawn had been taken out and replaced four times because Salina, my wife, wanted it to look better. Four different times it had been carefully rolled into place, carefully cut, carefully everything. And "carefully" meant expensive.

The brick planters along the front of the house always had to be perfect as well, present the perfect picture to the world of a happy, perfect home in our little subdivision. The perfect flowers had to be planted carefully in each planter for each of Portland, Oregon's seasons. Those flowers got replaced every two months, even if some of the old ones were still blooming.

And even worse, I had spent more money than I could ever imagine on slug poison because Salina had read an article about how slugs were bad in this part of the country.

Our lawn and planters, plus parts of the garage and the basement, were pure death to any poor slug that happened to wander into the yard. And who knew what all that poison was doing to other animals unlucky enough to venture across the line into Salina's perfect point-four acres in the suburbs.

Salina had loved her home, her yard, her plants, her furniture, her clothes, her dishes, her kitchen, everything she touched. She had tried to make everything perfect.

Even me.

But I was the one thing she could never make perfect, or convince to spend enough of my own money on myself to become what she considered perfect.

I was the one flaw in her perfectly ordered and maintained life.

She could spend my money on everything else, but I had drawn the line with changing myself.

And that had become our biggest problem. I just didn't care enough to be perfect. I kind of liked myself the way I was. I stood six-two, worked out so I had no excess weight at thirty-three, unlike most of my friends and co-workers in the law firm. And I had a smile that many said lit up a room.

But Salina said my nose was crooked and it needed to be

fixed. It was crooked, slightly, because of a skiing accident up on Mount Hood when I was twenty-four, a year after I married Salina. But I liked it. I thought it gave my face character.

Salina saw it as an imperfection.

And she was big into yoga, but no chance in hell I was going to do that. I ran in the gym down near the office and played golf in the summer and skied in the winter. No way I was going to sit and try to get my damned leg over my head.

Salina was into fine wines and had me spend a fortune for a wine cellar dug under the house. That cellar had been one of our biggest fights. Of course, she won.

The wine cellar was tighter than most bank vaults and controlled with its own environmental system. Expensive didn't begin to describe that room.

I hated most wines. I liked a good micro-brew and had a fridge in the perfectly clean garage that kept my beer.

And she had wanted me to learn to like the cultural stuff around Portland, but all I had wanted to attend was a University of Oregon Ducks football game.

So after years of marriage, I had become an abomination to Salina. She wouldn't allow me to touch her and she seldom talked to me unless she wanted something from me or wanted to criticize something I was doing, eating, or watching.

So today, as planned, I would end it.

If the plan worked as set out, Salina's little perfect world would come crashing down around her head.

I was in perfect form, ready to go on stage and play my part. It felt good to do this preparation time again.

I glanced up the street at the deep-blue convertible Cadillac parked like it belonged to the house three doors away. But Jimmy, my private detective and best friend, told me it belonged to Percy Samuels.

Salina and Percy.

Such a perfect-sounding couple.

Percy owned what seemed like a swank health spa in the Pearl District downtown, but Jimmy told me he was completely broke. Percy lived in a sloppy apartment littered with Coors beer cans and was within one month of having that fancy blue car repossessed.

On top of that, the IRS had liens on his business and were about to strike, a source told me.

That source, of course, was Jimmy.

Everything I knew about Salina and Percy came though Jimmy.

Jimmy and I had been friends since college and he knew how to dig out information in both legal and illegal ways. We skied together in the winter and played golf together every Saturday.

And now, with everything, we spent almost all our time together.

He only stood five-four, but was the most powerful small man I had ever met. I might be ten inches taller and weigh more, but not a chance in the world would I ever want to take him on in a fight.

Jimmy often found me information for a client I couldn't

legally use, but that illegal information usually pointed to something I could use.

Way back when I asked him to look into what Salina was doing, all he did was laugh. Then he said, "I was wondering when the sex was going to turn bad and you were going to grow a pair in dealing with her."

So Jimmy did his best and found all sorts of information that would allow me to kick Salina down the road and not pay her a cent.

Salina and Percy had been lovers now for six months. Usually in the afternoons when they knew I was going to be in court.

I had to admit, that was smart.

Of course, that backfired on them, all their careful planning.

And Salina had been stashing some cash away, which I had managed to make vanish out of her accounts.

Jimmy managed to get all our joint accounts locked down tight and all her credit cards cancelled.

Salina was as broke as her lover Percy.

I looked out over the perfect green lawn saturated in snail bait. It was time for me to play this game, walk on this stage, and go into that house once again. I already had a wonderful condominium downtown, only blocks from my office. And I liked it, had furnished it the way I wanted a place furnished, including the biggest screen one of the rooms could handle.

Percy and Salina were in their perfect world. They just didn't know it.

I almost felt sorry for him. Her, I never would have a moment's regret.

My cell phone in my pocket was on and open, connected to my best friend. "You there, Jimmy?"

"Waiting just around the corner as usual, Craig," Jimmy's deep voice came back strong. "Just leave the line open and I'll make sure I get everything. I'll come running if there is an ounce of trouble."

"Thanks, buddy," I said.

Jimmy played his part in our little play perfectly. You couldn't ask for a better friend.

Leaving the connection open in my pocket so that Jimmy could hear, I moved from the car and out into the sun.

For Portland, the day was warm, promising to top out in the mid-nineties.

Taking a deep breath to steady my nerves, just as I did when going into court, I moved up my front walk, my leather dress shoes making faint clicking sounds on the concrete that sounded like it echoed up and down the street.

I wasn't actually sure they made any sound, but I sure hoped they did, at least a little. In this play, I wanted them to make the noise.

Then, moving as silently as I could, I went through the front door and stood just inside. It felt like I was sweating slightly in the sudden coolness of the air. I wasn't sure if I actually was or if I just wanted to believe I was.

I had done it. I was inside.

I stayed very still to try to discover what I could hear.

Of course, there was nothing. I had done so much build-up to this, like planning a major court case, my nerves were almost out of control.

It made me feel alive, which I loved.

"You okay, Craig?" Jimmy's voice came faintly from my phone in my pocket.

I whispered. "Inside the house. Give me a minute."

The play continued.

I started down the hallway toward our master bedroom, working hard to make as little noise as possible.

No one there.

The huge room was in perfect condition, the bed made, the blinds open, the summer light filling the pink and orange space that was Salina's idea of a perfect master bedroom.

I felt dizzy, so I made myself take a couple deep breaths until the swirling passed. I couldn't let the images of anything but today come into my mind. I had to stay firmly in character or this would not work yet again.

After a moment, I went back to the game of searching for my wife and her lover, making sure I stayed right on the script Jimmy and I had worked out.

That was critical.

Of course I found nothing.

The house was empty.

I carefully opened a cabinet and took one of my old coffee mugs out and placed it on the counter, just where it wasn't supposed to be.

I stared at it for a moment, almost stunned, but again working to keep myself in character, acting as if what I had just done was perfectly normal.

Salina would have never allowed that to happen. It was something out of place, something not perfect, so if I left the mug there, she would have cleaned it up.

And then I would have heard about it for an hour.

"A place for everything and everything in its place," she would repeat over and over.

I tended to agree with that now for her.

I stared at the mug for a moment longer, savoring the victory.

Then I walked through the house again, looking in all four bedrooms, in my study, in her private room. Then I went down the narrow flight of stairs and into the wine cellar, making sure that I covered everything.

I had come to love the wine cellar and actually stood for a short time with one hand on the wine racks and just smiled at all the wine I had bought Salina that now she would never drink.

Then, as if I did the action every day, I took some slug bait from a trap in a back corner and spread it into the small wall heater. Then I turned on the wall heater.

It started to crackle. Perfect.

It worked.

I had managed to do at least that much this year.

I caught myself and made myself stay in perfect character for the play.

I continued my search.

No one.

The house had a feel of emptiness to it, and now that I was looking around again, I could see faint signs of dust in certain places.

The cleaning services were clearly not doing a good job.

I moved into the kitchen area and looked out over the living room. A very empty place, even though it was full of very expensive furniture.

I talked in the direction of my shirt pocket. "Jimmy, no one home."

"Be right there, buddy," he said and hung up.

I stood there on the edge of the living room staring around at the empty house with all the perfect furniture that had never felt like a home to me.

The play needed to continue.

Every detail needed to be perfect if this was to work. So I headed down the hall to make the motion of checking for her car. I had to stay on stage. That's what kept me grounded.

It was the only thing that mattered.

As I expected, her car was still parked there.

I went back to the dark granite kitchen counter as Jimmy came through the front door and moved over beside me.

He had a very worried look on his face.

I gave him a thumbs up and pointed to the mug.

"So where are they?" I asked him, indicating the empty room, continuing the script we had set up.

"Damn," Jimmy said. "I was so hoping that this year you would remember."

"Remember what?" I asked.

Jimmy started into his part of the script.

"Three years ago Salina and Percy figured out that you were going to kick her down the road. So they tried to poison you with slug bait."

I shook my head. I needed to pretend I had no memory of any of that. "What happened?"

"You managed to fight them off and get outside and call me and I managed to get you to a hospital. You were in a coma for almost four months."

I said nothing since I had no lines in this play and Jimmy went on talking, telling me a fantastic story that I knew wasn't possible.

Yet part of me wanted to believe it was possible, because it was such a nice story. A lot better than the truth I wanted to believe.

And a ton better than the real truth.

"When Salina and Percy realized you were going to live and they were going to be arrested, they made a run for Mexico. They didn't make it. She's still in jail in California for some crime they did down there and will be for another ten years before coming back up here to face charges for trying to kill you."

Jimmy could really tell a wild story and he had this one very well practiced after the years of telling it to me.

Again I said nothing, staying in the part of a person who couldn't remember anything that happened.

"When you woke up," Jimmy said, "you had only half your stomach left and no memory of anything. You were convinced instead that you and Salina were divorced and that she's completely gone. You just won't seem to believe anything else."

I would have never thought it would have been possible for Salina to try to kill me. I would have never thought the perfect woman in the perfect house with the perfect life had that sort of thing in her. Yet, in the real world, she got rid of everything that wasn't perfect or fixed it, so getting rid of me would have seemed logical to her.

It sure made for a great story for Jimmy to feed me to keep me on stage and solidly in this play.

Jimmy just went on telling me the story that he told me every year at this point. "You've kept this house perfect, just as Salina would have wanted it, even though you never come here except today. Every year, on this day, you come back here to tell her you are kicking her out. And I come with you to help."

I honestly loved this play. It was so real.

And Jimmy made his part of the story very convincing.

"And it happens like this every year?" I asked.

"Every damn year," Jimmy said, answering my question.

He was standing beside me, looking very worried.

"I think I'm going to be all right. The memories of the last few years seem to be coming back."

"Seriously?" Jimmy asked, his square face set in frown lines.

"Yup, I think I remember now," I said. "At least most of it. Still some foggy places."

Jimmy's large brown eyes just looked even more worried.

"So what do you remember?" Jimmy asked. "Everything. Run me through it."

And so the second act of our little play started.

Act Two

"I don't remember Salina serving me the slug bait," I said.

Again, this was just like being in a courtroom defending a client. My beliefs needed to be distant from my actions. I could never allow any belief but the belief I needed that day in court to come to the surface.

And that's the way I was playing this.

"I do remember a doctor telling me that the kind of coma I had gone into can cause some brain damage, especially to memory."

Jimmy nodded, staying on his part of the script and I could feel all this becoming solid and very real.

I smiled at my friend. "I remember you and I were planning on coming here later in the week to catch Salina and Percy doing the bed-sheet mambo and kick them out. But it never happened. Right?"

Jimmy nodded and said nothing.

I looked around the perfectly decorated big house.

And just like I was supposed to do in this part of the story, I did not mention to my best friend that Salina and Percy were behind the shelves in the wine cellar. That was the script. So I went along with the game he and I were playing to bring me back to the world.

We had tried this same game for the last couple years. Same game every year. Same script. We were getting better at it.

This very well might be the year.

"I have no memory of Salina being in jail however. Didn't she and Percy just vanish?"

"They did." Jimmy shrugged. "I've thought that they were better off gone from the start."

"But I do like the story of her being in jail," I said and Jimmy smiled.

If I really had memory issues.

As I did every year at this point in our little play, I asked the question once more. "Any idea where they are?"

Jimmy shook his head.

I looked around. "So why do I keep this place?"

Jimmy shrugged and said his lines perfectly. "Maybe it's because you think Salina and Percy might return if you keep it."

"That's just flat silly," I said, smiling at my friend and getting a smile in return.

I knew for a fact that they had never left.

"So you are making progress," Jimmy said.

"Real progress," I said.

I picked up the mug and put it back in the cabinet.

A place for everything and everything in its place.

Jimmy just nodded and smiled.

Salina and Percy were drinking wine naked the day I walked in on them, four days before I drank the slug poison to cover for me killing them, making people believe they had tried to kill me instead. She loved her wine cellar so much. She and her lover are now happy together down there.

A place for everything and everything in its place.

The wine cellar is a little smaller than it was originally designed, but I doubt anyone will notice.

"That's a hell of a story you tell me every year," I said to Jimmy, pretending I now remembered how much of a story it really was.

"I'll do anything to help," he said.

"Oh, you do help," I said.

And thus started the third act of our little play as we walked out into the afternoon sunshine.

Act Three

Salina and Percy were sitting there, in my car, Percy behind the steering wheel.

Right on schedule, as they always were. Salina did not believe in being late for anything.

I was now in perfect courtroom mode. I was deep in the belief of the case, knew what I had to believe and had tossed out all other beliefs. The ability to do that, stay completely submerged into the play in the courtroom, was why I had won so many cases.

After a moment Salina and Percy got out and started up

the walk toward the front door, neither saying a word to the other.

Clearly the sex was going bad between them and poor old Percy was starting to understand what kind of woman he had gotten hooked up with.

Jimmy and I stepped to one side and let them pass, then followed them back into the house.

We had done the same thing every year, but this year I hoped things would be different.

I made myself stop and not think that way. I needed to stay solidly on the script.

"So how come we just don't sell this place?" Percy asked. "We could sure use the money."

I was stunned. They had gone through most of my money and insurance in just three years. That was a lot of money.

I pushed that thought down as well and got back into my belief system.

Salina turned to him and gave him that nasty look she used to give me. "And have someone discover the bodies in the wine cellar?"

"That would be nice," I said.

Jimmy laughed.

Of course Salina and Percy didn't hear me. They just headed for the wine cellar.

Percy pulled the door open and said, "Wow, that's a smell."

Jimmy glanced at me and smiled. He knew at that moment that I had managed to get the slug bait on the heater and turn it on.

"It's in your head," Salina said, pushing past him and going down the stairs. "The bodies can't smell, you fool. We wrapped them up too tightly in layers of plastic and they are behind a very solid wall, remember?"

"How could I ever forget," Percy said, following her.

They went down the narrow stairs to check on where they had buried me and Jimmy behind the wine racks after killing us three years ago today.

I turned to my best friend. "I seemed to have left the door to the wine cellar open in my check of the house."

"Better close it," he said. "You know there are expensive bottles of wine down there you wouldn't want stolen."

So as if I was still playing the game of looking for Salina and her lover, I moved to the wine cellar door, pushed it closed, and locked it.

Everything in its place.

Then I turned off the lights and went to the breaker box and flipped the breaker switch, leaving the breaker for the heater down there on.

Jimmy just cheered beside me.

"Holy crap, we did it!" he shouted, jumping up and down in his excitement.

Actually, I was pretty stunned as well.

I could feel myself smiling and smiling.

The two people who had killed Jimmy and me were now locked with our bodies in the wine cellar in the dark.

And they were breathing very poison air.

A moment later I could hear Percy banging on the door

shouting to be let out. His voice did not sound like he was much in control.

Behind him I heard Salina coughing. Then she said, "Idiot! Why did you pull the door closed behind you?"

"I didn't," Percy said, his voice a couple octaves higher than normal.

Salina coughed a few more times, then said, "Break it down, you fool."

The door pounded hard, but I remembered that when we had that wine cellar built, Salina wanted the best material and the best locks since we were going to have a lot of expensive wine down there.

She had said that many, many times to me during construction and in the arguments leading up to construction.

So the door held and then after a moment there was a loud crashing sound as two bodies tumbled back down the stairs.

And then it was silent.

"I'll be," Jimmy said, laughing. "We did it! We actually did it!"

I could feel this immense sense of satisfaction. Three years of practicing the scripts to make sure I felt connected to the real world. Three years of returning here to this house I hated on the day she had killed me and my best friend. We had caught her making love to Percy, but we didn't expect the gun she had bought and had in the drawer beside her.

And I didn't know about her trips to the gun range to learn how to use the thing.

Three years waiting for revenge.

And now it was here.

Outside I could hear the faint sounds of a siren headed this way.

"She got off a 911 call," Jimmy said, suddenly looking worried again.

"They won't be alive by the time the police find them," I said, smiling at my best friend.

"I hope you are right," he said.

"I am," I said. "Head back to your waiting spot for a minute, would you? We need to start the play over just one more time. I want to make sure they find our bodies as well."

He looked puzzled, but just nodded and then vanished.

A moment later his voice came over my phone inside my suit coat. "I'm here if you need me."

I said in the general direction of my pocket, "Listen and enjoy."

I put myself back in the courtroom, back in the belief that I was alive and could actually move physical objects without thinking about it.

I believed it more than I had ever believed in a case.

I was here to look for Salina and Percy in bed together.

I looked around the home I hated, then moved over to the front door and opened it and left it standing open for Jimmy to come in. Just in case I had trouble when I found Salina and Percy in bed together.

Staying solidly in my belief of where and when I was, I went back through the house, looking for Salina and her boyfriend. Making sure that with every thought, every belief, I would find them alive and making love.

Of course, I didn't find them.

As I finished my search of the back bedrooms, I heard a call from the front door. "Police! Anyone here?"

I had heard no sounds at all from the wine cellar in almost five minutes. So on the way toward the front I clicked back on the breaker lights for the wine cellar.

Then focusing as hard as I could to stay in the act of our little play and not get caught for murdering my wife and her lover and putting their bodies behind the wine racks, I went forward to greet the police.

I had to play this one perfectly. Just like a summary statement in front of a jury.

I had done it a thousand times. Once more, with flourish this time.

"Hello," I said and two young cops both turned to me.

Wow, they were making patrol officers young these days. Both looked like they were right out of college, if that. One even had a face of pimples.

I pointed at the door just off the kitchen. "My wife and her boyfriend are dead down there in the wine cellar."

They both just looked at me, clearly stunned and trying to process what I had just said. Then the one with the bad skin said, "Did you do it?"

What a stupid question for a policeman to ask, but I was glad he did. He played right into my plan perfectly.

"Of course I did," I said. "I killed them. But there are

two bodies behind one of the wine racks that she killed. Make sure you take care of those as well."

Then, while they stood there stunned, I walked for the last time out the front door of the house Salina built and I had come to hate.

"Hey, wait a minute!" one cop said behind me and turned to follow.

But I was gone.

"Where did he go?" the one cop asked.

Quickly they went in different directions around the house, looking for me while calling in for backup.

But they would never find me, at least this part of me. I hoped they found my body down there behind the wine rack.

But this part of me was back in my reality. I was off stage, out of the belief that I had needed to touch the few things I had needed to touch. I knew and believed now that I was only a ghost.

And beside me, Jimmy was laughing.

"Well played," he said. "Who knew you could act like that."

"I'm a trial lawyer, remember," I said. "I can believe anything if I really need to."

"Oh, yeah," he said. "Who would have thought as a ghost I would need a lawyer."

Laughing, we turned and walked down Bryant Street.

I had no idea where we were going, but anywhere was better than staying in that home with that woman.

USA *Today* Bestselling Writer
DEAN WESLEY SMITH

THE MAN WHO USED SHRILL WHISPERS
A Bryant Street Story

BRYANT STREET

THE MAN WHO USED SHRILL WHISPERS

Bryant Street exists in that subdivision where reality tips over into the absurd.

Accountant Frank Filby and his one special skill live on Bryant Street. He knows everything about everyone in the entire subdivision. Keeps track.

Frank thinks of himself as the god of the subdivision.

Another twisted Bryant Street story where reality sometimes means little.

Frank Filby had a talent.

Or a skill.

Or maybe it could be called a gift. He didn't know. Early in life he had considered his talent, his gift, a curse and his mother had tried to cure him of it by first beating him and then taking him to doctors for drugs.

All it cured him of was talking about what he could do.

Frank Filby could hear the thoughts of someone in emotional pain. That was his gift.

It seemed everyone had emotional pain.

He called what he heard a shrill whisper.

Shrill because emotional pain always seemed shrill to Frank. Whisper because that was what the thoughts from others sounded like to him inside his own head.

Now, at the age of thirty-five, Frank lived alone in a three-bedroom ranch on a suburban street smack in the middle of a subdivision with exactly one thousand, two hundred and seven homes, his home not included.

Simply driving out of the subdivision to get to a local grocery store took him numbers of twists and turns that confused many, but that he knew by heart.

For a living, Frank worked alone, in an office in his home, doing online accounting. He was good at it and had steady clients that kept his bills paid and extra legal, taxable money building up in his many bank accounts.

During week-day business hours, even at home, Frank wore a dress shirt with a blue bowtie, brown slacks and comfortable loafers. His hair was thin and he kept it trimmed close to his head. He stood five-ten and was very thin, even though he ate three meals a day.

After hours and on weekends he wore a darker blue long-sleeved dress shirt and darker slacks and tennis shoes.

To a stranger coming in, Frank's home looked perfectly

maintained and cleaned and he never left dishes out in the sink or clothes anywhere but in his walk-in closet where he dressed every day.

Strangers never came into Frank's house. In fact, since he had bought the house ten years earlier with an inheritance from his mother's estate, no one had ever been inside his home.

His business office was in a small bedroom to the right of the simple living room. The office had a simple wooden desk, a simple chair, and a computer with a printer and scanner.

A few accounting and business and tax books filled a small bookcase under the room's only window.

The living room had a reading chair, a long brown cloth couch, and a large-screen television facing the couch.

He watched news every night from three channels and nothing else. He loved the news for all the stories about all the ugly things humans were capable of doing.

He read only books about human nature, human psychology, and human feelings. Those books were his passion because they helped him understand his gift better. The few hundred books that he owned on that topic were arranged neatly on a large bookshelf unit on one wall behind his reading chair.

Every night, just after the sun had set, Frank went for a walk.

The subdivision had wonderful sidewalks and Frank made sure to smile at anyone he saw during his nightly walk. Neighbors even waved at him. He found that ironic.

Over the course of two weeks, he walked in front of every home in the subdivision. Then he would start the pattern over.

He had been doing this for ten years.

He had never missed a night no matter the temperature or weather.

In what would have been a family room in his house, behind a locked door, Frank had a large map of the subdivision on a wall.

Every house was numbered and in a large file cabinet beside the map was a numbered folder for every house.

A massive oak desk sat in the middle of the room facing the map and two large-screen computers sat on the desk. A high-backed leather office chair sat behind the desk.

Here, at this desk, after he came home from his walk, Frank recorded the information his gift had brought to him.

The file on each home in the subdivision contained exact information about each resident in the home. Names, likes, dislikes, birthdays, social security numbers, bank account numbers.

Everything.

And most importantly what each person in each home liked, hated, was feeling, and wanting.

And all the misdeeds of each person as well in the house, from the petty to the large.

His gift allowed him to listen to the close emotional thoughts of a person inside a house as he walked by.

He could listen to their shrill whispers and learn everything about them.

And sometimes he did something about what he heard. Mostly he just listened and recorded in the files.

Mostly.

At least at first.

As the years had gone by, Frank found himself thinking he was like a god of the subdivision, an all-powerful, all-seeing entity that knew every secret, every lie, every small detail of every person who lived in his subdivision world.

And over the last few years he had started to use that information in various ways, often to solve a problem which created more emotional stress that then allowed him to enjoy his gift better. This week he had sent blackmail e-mails to five husbands and six wives in the subdivision.

Those e-mails were what he called his "monthly affair tax" for those having an affair and living in his subdivision. He considered an affair a petty crime, so he charged them accordingly.

Each e-mail had been from an untraceable address, even by the best hacker, and he told each person to give exactly three thousand dollars to a charity account of their choice and send him a copy of the receipt. Otherwise he would tell the partner or spouse of the affair.

He never kept the "monthly affair tax" for himself.

But he did enjoy the extreme emotional turmoil the letters always caused, which made his walks past that house even more enjoyable for a few months.

Extreme emotional stress made a person's thoughts clear as a bell to him. Their whispers almost became like clear conversations over a phone.

Every night after his walk, he came back refreshed, feeling charged as he recorded every detail in the files.

Twice in the last year he had managed to stop a wife beater and once two years before he had stopped a wife from killing her husband. Both times he had done it through very detailed, anonymous tips to the police.

Six times in the last year he had stopped child abuse. He loved bathing in the emotional torture of an adult, but children were off limits as far as he was concerned. His mother had done enough damage to him.

For the child abusers in the family, the worst crime there was as far as he was concerned, he had a very simple solution. He killed them, just as he had killed his mother. Not in exactly the same way, of course, but in creative ways for each one.

Last month, for the abuser named Harry three streets over at 2910 Harper, Frank had simply hacked into his computer and put on his screen a subliminal flashing image that repeated to Harry that he was a worthless human being over and over and should take the gun in his closet and blow his brains out.

It took two weeks, but finally Harry did, leaving child porn up on his computer for everyone to see.

For the white-collar criminals who cheated at their work, Frank simply took their money, moving it from their bank accounts to his when it was the most incriminating for them.

And what Frank found most interesting is that by all national statistics, this subdivision had no higher or lower crime rate than any other. Frank often wondered if there were others like him, gods of neighborhoods, keeping the world a better place to live.

He hoped so. But he had no desire to meet any of them.

But as with many gods, Frank had a weakness.

He didn't know he did until four months after Johnny Aimes moved into a house five doors down from Frank.

Johnny's house, also on Bryant Street as was Frank's home, was along Frank's walking route to get to a larger part of the subdivision.

So Frank walked past Johnny's home five nights per week.

Johnny was also an accountant, a man with serious computer skills and very, very little emotional issues. Johnny was two inches taller than Frank and had short hair. He kept his new home looking perfect from the outside, as Frank did with his.

Frank had very, very little information on Johnny since the man seemed to just be serene. Without emotional distress, Frank could not get any shrill whispers from Johnny.

Then four months in, Frank got a sense that something was causing Johnny some distress.

And it took Frank two nights of walking past Johnny's home to discover from the whispers that the cause of the distress was Frank himself.

Johnny was in lust with Frank.

Johnny had seen Frank on his nightly walks, waved at Frank a few times and Frank had smiled at him. And now

Johnny was working to stop himself from imagining Frank without clothes on.

And fighting to keep himself from going to the window to watch Frank walk past.

At first, Frank had laughed that off, but as Johnny's emotional distress got stronger over the lust, Frank could read his mind and see the images very clearly.

Disturbing images, yet erotic images. Frank had never felt that directed at him and he honestly didn't know what to do.

Johnny had investigated Frank, knew that he was single, that he worked at home, and that he had never been married.

Those details had excited Johnny even more and now he was working on a way to actually meet Frank and talk with him.

Until Frank had discovered that Johnny's imaginations were erotic, Frank had never considered himself a sexual being in any way. But clearly if he leaned at all, it was toward another man.

And Johnny's mind was giving Frank a clear roadmap of what that kind of relationship would be like.

Then one fine evening, in the middle of one of Johnny's elaborate fantasies about himself and Frank, Johnny slipped. He dropped his mental guard slightly, just enough to let Frank catch a glimpse in Johnny's mind of the real intent.

Johnny had the same talent as Frank.

Exactly.

The sex stuff had all been a ruse to try to disrupt Frank.

And Frank had been an open book to Johnny with each night's walk. Frank being conflicted on the sexual interest had allowed Johnny to get into Frank's mind.

Frank continued on his walk as if nothing was wrong, blocking Johnny from any access besides the surface of Frank's brain. Once Frank was back at home, he checked all his computers.

Only his accounting office computer had been compromised. More than likely Johnny hadn't got deep enough yet in Frank's mind to see his real office in the old family room.

But Frank checked every detail just in case.

Clean.

Then, carefully, very carefully, he explored into Johnny's computer, and found fairly quickly that Johnny had a second computer as well.

And that was when Frank got the shock of his life. Johnny had been in contact with an organization of others like Frank, others who could read minds, who controlled areas like this subdivision all over the world.

They controlled massive corporations and governments as well.

Actually, from everything Frank could tell with careful searches over a few days, the main corporation behind everything called itself Deep Water Lives, Inc. It was a huge corporation and they had noticed that the normal crime rates were slightly off in this subdivision.

Frank had started involving himself in other people's lives instead of just watching. That had been his mistake.

They had discovered Frank ten months earlier, which shocked Frank more than he wanted to admit. He had been so very, very careful.

But not careful enough and that was why Johnny was here. They had sent Johnny to either bring Frank into the organization or to deal with him.

Frank was not a joiner. He was a god of his own world and that was exactly how he wanted to remain.

He had no desire to be some corporate lackey standing where he was told and doing what he was told.

So making sure to keep his mind blocked completely, he stayed in his routine for the next week while planning his next move. Turned out his move was simple.

He sent an e-mail to the president of Deep Water Lives, Inc., and the chairman of the board. If they did not back away and pull Johnny from the subdivision, Frank would ignite every gas line in the entire subdivision and blow the entire place off the map.

Frank could do that. Easily.

From his laptop while sitting two miles away.

And the people in charge of Deep Water Lives knew Frank could do that.

Johnny was loading things into an SUV the next evening when Frank walked past.

Johnny nodded to Frank.

Frank smiled and waved back.

Frank's problem was solved.

He was again the god of his own world. All powerful.

Six nights later, what appeared to be a stray bullet from

a nearby robbery gone bad, struck Frank between the eyes while he was on his walk.

When the police went into Frank's home the next day, they found only a regular family room where Frank's planning room used to be.

Frank was buried without anyone attending his funeral under the conditions of his will and his money went to charities.

A god had died, but no one on Bryant Street knew it or cared.

Two weeks later Johnny moved back into the house he had just left and a month later started regular exercise runs around the Bryant Street subdivision.

And the balance in the subdivision remained.

USA *Today* Bestselling Writer

DEAN WESLEY SMITH

She Took And Took
Until He Said, "No More."

AN OBSCENE CRIME
AGAINST PASSION

BRYANT STREET

AN OBSCENE CRIME AGAINST PASSION

James Ward no longer cares what his wife does in her spare time. He no longer cares about anything, actually.

Deborah took his passion over years. Drained him until he could give no more.

But on Bryant Street, sick relationships often reveal hidden secrets.

Passion functions as a food for some, energy for others. But who knows what role passion plays on Bryant Street.

ONE

The night James Ward finally confronted his wife for what she truly was started when police car lights flashed outside the large picture window of his suburban home. The drawn cloth curtains kept most of the light out, as well as the closed blinds under the curtains, but he still noticed the blue-red combination.

He couldn't remember the last time he had opened those windows and unless he heard shots out there in the cul-de-sac, he wasn't opening them now. The last baseball games before the All-Star break were being played tonight and he wanted to make sure he caught as many of them as he could.

He glanced around at his two-bedroom ranch-style home from his favorite recliner wondering where Deborah had gone. Over the last few years they had just drifted into doing their own things in their own ways at their own times.

The marriage had become convenient for both of them, passion a thing of the past, as he had expected would happen when they married but had hoped would not happen, as any newlywed hopes.

His life now was working at the insurance agency and watching baseball and doing a little betting on games down at the local casino. And just waiting. He did not expect his wait to end right before the All-Star Break in baseball.

He honestly had no idea what Deborah's interests had become as they drifted apart. She said she did some teaching, but he didn't remember what type or when or where.

And he honestly didn't care. Sad, considering she was his wife.

James was a tall, handsome man, at least many said that,

and did some minor exercise to stay in shape. Deborah was just as stunningly beautiful now as the day he met her.

Everyone who saw them together said they made a perfect couple.

If they only knew.

Suddenly, just as the two teams were returning to the field after the seventh inning to finish up the nine-one disaster-of-a-game he had been watching, a loud banging at the front door shook the house.

"Deborah!" he shouted.

No response.

More banging.

"All right, all right," he said, climbing out of his recliner and heading for the door.

On the front porch stood two police officers. One a man, one a woman. The woman cop had a hooker by the arm and the hooker was turned away from the porch light.

He had no idea why cops would bring a hooker to his door at eight in the evening on a weeknight.

The cops were dressed in standard city cop uniforms and the hooker had on a very, very short skirt that barely covered the bottom of her ass, a mesh blouse that you could see through, torn black stockings, and heels so high that they looked more like stilts than shoes.

Women like her often walked along some of the worst streets downtown. He always avoided those areas. He just wasn't interested.

"You James Ward?" the guy asked.

"Yeah," James said.

"You married to Deborah Ward?" the guy asked.

"I am," James said. "Is she all right?"

"She seems to be," the cop said, handing James a small purse. "But might want to get her some help."

"And keep her off the streets," the woman cop said. "Dangerous downtown."

With that, the woman cop turned the hooker around and pushed her toward the door.

The hooker nodded to James and walked past him into the house, taking the small purse out of his hands as she went.

The cops both nodded to James without smiling and turned back toward their car as James stood there, surprised that the night had finally arrived.

It seemed events had transpired to move his life forward.

Finally, he slowly backed into the house and closed the door.

Then he turned around.

Deborah, his wife of five years, dressed like a twenty-dollar streetwalker, stood there, facing him. Her makeup was almost so thick as to crack and her normally wonderful brown hair had been greased back off her face.

"Surprise, huh?" she said, then popped some gum.

He opened his mouth, but said nothing.

Nothing.

"Let me go take a hot shower, get into my normal costume, and then we can talk," she said. "Be a sweetie and fix me a Bloody Mary. All the fixings are in the cabinet above the fridge where you would never look. It was a bitch of a night out there."

With a practiced ease on the extremely tall heels, she turned and headed back toward her closet and bedroom.

All James could do was stand there and watch her ass sway under her tight, short skirt as she went down the hall. That was an amazing costume she was wearing.

Then he went over and turned off the game and headed for the kitchen.

With this, he was going to need a drink as well.

Maybe two. If the night turned out as he hoped it would.

TWO

The kitchen of their suburban home was everything Deborah had wanted when they moved in. White modern cabinets, granite countertops, a dark floor, and modern stainless appliances.

The entire house had been remodeled. Some of it to her wants, a lot to his hidden reasons.

On the way to the kitchen he clicked a few hidden switches that would help him with the evening to come.

The kitchen table was custom-made to fit the space and could hold six, but since neither of them had much in the way of friends, that table had usually seated only the two of them. And their formal dining room had never been used.

Just wasn't either of their styles or their natures to have friends.

James hadn't objected to anything she had added in the remodel as long as it made her smile. When they were first married five years ago, he had loved to see her smile.

She had been fun to watch.

And they had made love regularly, in all sorts of ways. He liked that more than he wanted to admit.

That had ended slowly over the first year.

James dug out the glasses, the Bloody Mary mix, the vodka, and even a couple sticks of celery from the fridge he hadn't noticed before. He normally drank beer and didn't much like vegetables.

He put her drink in front of her chair and sat down in his chair and sipped on his drink, stirring it with the celery.

Since he had spent so much time at the casino lately in the sports book, he and Deborah had taken to eating meals on their own.

Now that he thought about it, the only thing they had left in their marriage was this house. Wow, that was sad.

But it felt more like a fact to him than a sadness. He had hoped for something more. Sure.

But it hadn't happened.

Shouldn't he be angry at all this? At her hooking downtown? At her sleeping with who knew how many other men?

A normal husband would.

He tried to think back. He couldn't remember the last time he had gotten angry about anything. It had been a very long time.

He didn't even get that much of a thrill with winning a

bet and didn't get angry either with losing. Gambling used to make him feel alive.

Wow, he had become a dead shell in this marriage. How pathetic was that?

He needed new energy, new focus, new everything. Looked like after tonight he was finally going to get it.

After a few minutes, Deborah came out wearing her blue bathrobe and slippers. Her hair was wet and pulled back and her face looked like it had been scrubbed pretty well to get the makeup off.

She didn't even look close to the same woman who had walked through the front door thirty minutes ago. This was the Deborah he had married.

She sat down and took a pretty good drink of her Bloody Mary, then sat back with a sigh.

"Thanks, I needed that."

He nodded and took another drink as well.

Then he looked at her. "How long have you been doing this?"

She laughed. "If you mean being a prostitute, since I was fifteen. I was trained by my mother."

Again his mouth opened and yet not a word came out.

Nothing.

There was just nothing he could say to that as her husband.

Finally, he just shook his head and took another sip of his drink. A normal husband with a normal wife would be furiously angry at all this, at being lied to, at everything.

But he wasn't.

He couldn't be and he actually didn't feel a thing, as she knew would be the case.

She stared at him for a moment, then seemed to finally take pity on him, as he had been hoping for five years she would do.

"Have you ever met a person who just seemed to suck the life out of a room?" she asked.

He nodded. "Numbers of them back in college. There is a guy by the name of Hank in our office that does the same thing at times."

"You ever wonder where that life goes?" she asked.

He looked into her deep brown eyes and could see her question was serious. She was going to finally tell him the truth.

About damned time. Way too late, however.

"You ever heard of vampires?" she asked.

He nodded.

"Vampires in fiction survive from taking the life force, blood, out of others."

He nodded. He had seen his share of bad movies.

"Blood vampires do not exist," she said, matter-of-factly, looking at him and seeming to hold him.

"But energy eating beings do exist," she said. "They are ancient humans that need the energy, the passion, the life force of normal humans to exist. I am one of them. We call ourselves Primals."

The truth was finally out.

Finally.

The cop had been right, she really did need help. Just not the help the cop had intended.

"Have you been wondering why you feel nothing anymore about anything and are not angry right now about your wife being a hooker?"

He nodded, going with her. "That has bothered me."

"I keep you drained of that sort of energy," she said. "It's why you took that dull job, bet on sports without any thrill of winning or worry about losing, and why we stopped having sex a long time ago."

"You keep me drained?" he asked. "Why would you do that?"

"Because for the next fifteen or twenty years, I needed what we Primals call a cow. You, my sweet James, are my cow."

Damn he wanted to get angry, but just nothing came up.

"What exactly is the function of a cow?" he asked.

"I will not age," she said, "so for the next fifteen or so years, until our age difference starts to get noticed, you will supply me with a base level of energy, passion, joy, enough for me to survive for weeks at a time without being around others."

She was taking his joy, his energy, his caring, as he knew she was. As he had known it from the moment he tracked her down and got close to her, let her feel his energy.

"So why are you hooking?" he asked, sipping on his Bloody Mary.

"Once a week I need the boost, the thrill of sex with

strangers, the fear that goes with that sex, the passion of men not used to feeling passion."

"You drain them all?" he asked.

"In a matter of speaking," she said, smiling. "Yes. They feel empty, calm, and without guilt when they leave me."

"So why me?" he asked.

He knew the answer. But now that her truth was out in the air between them, he wanted to hear her say it.

She smiled at him. A cold smile as only a Primal can give, but a real smile.

"Because I love you," she said. "And I wanted to spend a couple decades with you."

"Until I die from lack of energy," he said.

She nodded. "Pretty much."

He knew that wasn't going to happen. And it really made him sad to hear her say that. He had hoped for a different result.

"So are you going to keep hooking?" he asked. "That seems like a rather risky thing to continue to do after tonight, now that your name is on file with the police."

He was actually very glad she had slipped up and her name was on file as a hooker. It would make the next things he had to do even easier.

"I was thinking we need to have your brother come live with us," she said. "We have two spare rooms. Maybe he and his wife could both come. That would be fun for me."

He looked at her, knowing exactly what she was planning, but still playing along. "I don't have a brother."

"Of course you don't," she said, laughing. "I'll find us

one, maybe a couple, and get us a cover story. It will be far more fun for a few years than walking those streets in those heels."

He just shook his head. So now he was going to share Deborah with two other people.

It seemed time to end this.

He sipped on his Bloody Mary, then looked up at her and smiled. "Ever hear of a group called Libertas?"

Her face drained of the freshly-washed look. Her eyes darted from one side to the other, clearly looking for a way to run.

There was no way.

He had made this house a perfect Primal trap and he had turned on that trap while she was in the shower.

"You didn't answer my question," he said.

"Libertas is a group of hunters that survive on finding and draining Primals such as myself."

She looked at him, really looked at him. "Are you a Libertas?"

"Of course I am," he said, laughing. "When I saw you that first day we met in the supermarket, your arrogance of just brushing men and draining them, I knew I could easily convince you I could be a perfect cow."

Her eyes flashed in anger. But then that anger faded and her skin got pale.

He sipped on his Bloody Mary as she slowly realized what was happening to her. He was draining her energy into the fields surrounding the house. And the house was then feeding him that energy through his chair.

She tried to stand, to run, but it was too late. She didn't have the energy left in her body for even that much.

A couple hundred years ago, he would have had to fight and kill her in a bloody fashion, cutting off her head and everything.

But with the modern science at his disposal, he could build a trap that would pull the energy from her.

A lot better than cutting off her head.

"How did you keep yourself hidden from me?" she asked, her voice weakening.

"Your arrogance," he said. "You never thought to look and I played your cow perfectly, didn't I? When a hunter starts to believe they cannot be beat, then the hunted have a clear advantage."

She could no longer hold up her head and she slumped to the table.

He could see her clear, wonderful skin start to wrinkle and become brittle just as if she were an old woman.

"And just so you know," he said. "I loved you as well. And if you hadn't wanted me to be your cow, we could have had a great and long life together."

She didn't have the energy to say anything, but she did acknowledge that she had heard him by raising a few fingers.

He sat back, sipping his Bloody Mary, letting the energy she had in her body pour through the house and into him. For the first time in years, he again felt alive.

He had won the fight and another Primal would soon be gone from the planet. And that was worth a drink over.

He kept sipping on his Bloody Mary, watching as his wife of five years shrunk up more and more.

She now no longer had the capability to even move.

Her energy that was pouring through the house to him would keep him alive for decades to come. Because just as Primals, Libertas also were immortal. Only they did not feed off the helpless, they fed from Primals.

He had been doing so for more centuries than he wanted to remember.

She never knew in five years that while she was taking surface, human energy from him, he was pulling deeper energy from her. More than likely that was why she had decided to go find others. She didn't get enough from him because he took almost as much from her as she took from him.

It had been a perfect balance.

Many would say a perfect marriage.

Finally, her body broke apart, mostly into dust as the house kept sucking every last bit of life energy from her.

"It was an interesting five years, Deborah," he said, raising his glass in a toast. "I can't say you were a worthy opponent. But for a while there, the sex was great."

And it had been, which should have clued her to what he really was.

Energy between a Primal and a Libertas in sex could be almost explosive, since they fed back and forth off each other, sometimes cycling energy up into mind-blowing events.

They had had a few such events right before and right

after they were married, but she considered them only the passion of their newlywed moments.

And she had always considered him nothing more than a cow.

He had known better.

And just as with every time he married a Primal, he had hoped she would love him enough to not turn him into a cow.

But in thousands of years of marriages now, that had never happened.

But someday he would find the Primal of his dreams. And she would not turn him into a cow, not want to turn him into a cow, and he would not end up killing her for her greed.

A fella could only hope.

Across from him, the dust that had been Deborah just slowly settled onto the chair and on the floor.

Every bit of life energy she had was now his.

He finished his drink and went to get the vacuum cleaner.

And to see who had ended up winning that last baseball game.

BRYANT STREET

USA *Today* Bestselling Writer

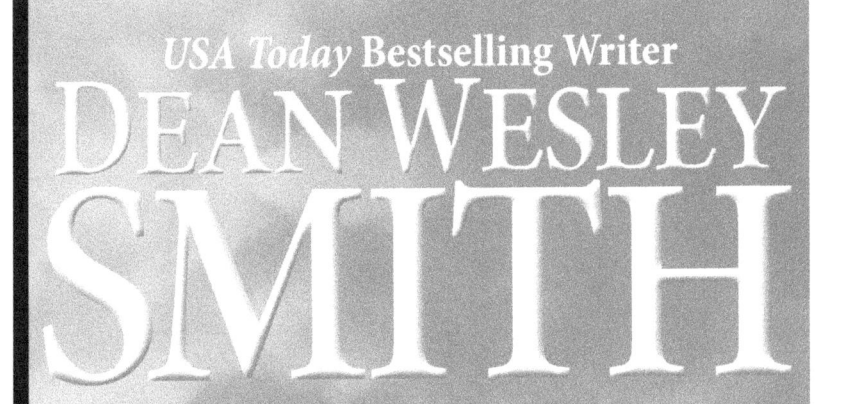

DEAN WESLEY SMITH

THEY WERE DIVIDED BY COLD DEBT

A Bryant Street Story

BRYANT STREET

THEY WERE DIVIDED BY COLD DEBT

Bryant Street, a standard subdivision street, haunts us all. To escape Bryant Street often takes real courage.

Meet Neil Prendell. He made a mistake. He lost his job but avoided telling his wife. Instead, he pretended to go to work while looking for another job.

Pride? Fear? Stupidity? The reason no longer mattered. He paid the price. A price that only made sense in the twisted logic of Bryant Street.

ONE

The mailboxes in his section of the Wilderness Park Subdivision all had stylized images of beavers on them cut out of metal. Every section of the subdivision had different animals on the mailboxes. And every mailbox was the same, just with slightly different numbers on their sides.

Every day that Neil Prendell drove off to his pretend job, he shook his head at the rows of identical metal beavers perched on top of the boxes as they mocked him.

And every day when he came home, they mocked him again.

It didn't help that he was coming home from a day of sitting in three different coffee shops searching for any possible job. He wasn't the only one in those shops searching, and he doubted he was the only lonely, desperate soul at those tables who hadn't told his wife that he had lost his job.

Times were bad for jobs.

Real bad.

Especially middle-management like him. His main skill was saying yes to one person and bossing others under him around. And he wasn't even that good at that, even with his MBA.

His goal had always been to be a guitar player in a band, but in the last year he hadn't even picked up his guitar.

He just didn't dare tell his wife Pam about losing his job. He had thought at first, he would find another one quickly and then tell her. In ten years of marriage, this home among the metal beavers had been the first time she had really been happy with him. Before he seemed to always not be good enough in her eyes.

And it had been her idea they both get MBAs. They had met in college when he was a music major. Her interest had always gone to real estate, but she had never really gotten the chance since college to work in the field. And now, with the recession hitting the housing so hard, he doubted she could find work either, even if she started looking.

So if he couldn't find another job and quickly, they would lose the house.

Lose their own very special beaver on the mailbox.

And more than likely, he would lose Pam. And he would deserve it. She was going to be so angry at him for not telling her and letting the situation get so bad. They had always split the finances. But when they bought the house, they had just moved the payments into the accounts he managed and she had taken the household accounts to run.

Even though she had quit her job a year ago at a major supply office to study for the real estate license exam and just hadn't taken it yet, he still loved her more than he wanted to think about. He didn't know what she did all day while he was job searching, but that didn't stop his love for her.

After two coffee shops today, he had finally gained a backbone. It was only two in the afternoon and he was headed home to finally tell her the problem.

Maybe together they could get through this because he was having no luck on his own. The debts were just too much.

He had never gone home in the middle of the afternoon before. Never.

His schedule was very regulated in his old job and Pam knew that.

The subdivision looked awfully quiet at this time of the day.

Every house in this area of the subdivision had been built off of five basic models, all two stories tall with wood shingles. All paint colors and any kind of landscaping had to be approved by the homeowners association from a very narrow list. The paints were all soft blues, tans, and greens. Very soft.

Boring soft.

Amazing how seeing a neighborhood in the cold light of financial ruin could make it look so different.

And he hated the beavers even more now.

But Pam loved the house and the entire neighborhood and she thought the beavers cute. To Neil the entire place felt more and more every day like a jail cell, with rows of metal beavers as his jailers.

Finally, after almost three months, on this beautiful spring day, he had decided to tell her. They were now over two months behind on their mortgage and about to fall into foreclosure. And he had maxed their credit cards on gas and other things for the house.

He had no choice. He would have to take the risk of losing her.

And losing all the rows of beavers as well.

He would miss Pam with all his heart if she left him. And he wouldn't blame her if she did. He had made a horrid and stupid blunder.

But he wouldn't miss the beavers.

TWO

As he headed down the street toward his home, he noticed three For Sale signs on lawns. And numbers of other houses looked empty.

One had a bank foreclosure sign on it.

Clearly he wasn't the only one in beaver land to be having problems.

There were very few cars in the driveways along the street since most of the homeowners were off at work and at this time of the day in the spring, the kids were all still in school. Luckily, he and Pam had no kids.

A blue Mercedes sedan sat in front of his house as he pulled into the driveway. Suddenly his mind spun out of control.

Was Pam having an affair on him?

When he asked her what she did all day, she had always avoided the question with just "Worked around the house."

Of course, when she asked him how the job was going, he just had avoided the question like she had.

It seemed their marriage had been built on distrust for some time now. How had it gotten down to that? At one point they had been the power couple among their friends, the two that would take over the world.

Now they couldn't even make a mortgage payment.

Or tell each other the truth.

He pulled into the driveway and instead of hitting the garage door opener, he just parked and got out into the warm afternoon air and closed his car door quietly.

He could smell the scent of freshly mowed grass and in the distance he could hear a leaf blower.

With his key in hand, he went to the front door and quietly opened it and stepped inside.

Pam's laugh came from the kitchen.

He loved her laugh, but at this moment, hearing that laugh, he almost turned and left. He didn't want to confront what he might see if he went around that corner into the dining room.

Just as he hadn't wanted to confront Pam when he lost his job.

It seems he was a coward, a lot more than he had ever thought of himself as one before.

When had he become so afraid?

He took a deep breath and stepped into the dining area that was beside the large, modern kitchen that Pam loved so much. The house smelled of bacon, so she must have cooked herself a bacon and cheese sandwich for lunch. She loved those as well.

Pam's eyes actually brightened as she saw him and she smiled and stood up from where she sat across from a man in a blue casual shirt. Pam had on her tan slacks and a white blouse and tan jacket, with earrings. She looked like she had just come home from an office.

She came over and kissed him hard, then smiled and turned. "Neil, I want you to meet Karl Benson. Karl, this is my husband Neil."

"I've heard a lot about you," Karl said, standing and

moving to shake Neil's hand. "Great to finally meet you and get you on board all this."

Neil shook his hand, putting on his company face, the one that tried not to show his complete bafflement at the situation.

On the counter where Karl and Pam had sat were folders and a lot of papers.

"What are you two up to?" Neil asked, nodding at the papers.

"Just some work I've been meaning to tell you about," Pam said, smiling at Karl and moving back to the counter.

She gathered up a few of the papers, then looked up at Karl. "Mind if I keep these for the evening and show Neil?"

"Not at all," Karl said. "See you at the Morrison property around ten tomorrow morning?"

"Sounds perfect," Pam said. "We'll be there."

Karl turned to Neil and smiled. "Wonderful to finally put a face to the name. See you tomorrow."

And with that, he headed out.

Neil watched him go, then turned back to Pam who had finished straightening up the piles of papers and had them stacked in neat, clearly labeled folders.

"So what's going on?" Neil asked.

"I'll explain it all in a minute, but first I want to know if you found a job? Is that why you are home early?"

Neil sort of rocked back. "You knew?"

She laughed and came over and kissed him. "Of course I knew and I also knew how hard you were looking for a new one. It was boneheaded for you to keep it from me, but

I loved you for trying to protect me like that. Very macho in a 1950s sitcom fashion."

He laughed, letting the feeling of relief spread through his body. "Stupid was what it was."

"Note that you said that and I didn't disagree," she said. "So, did you find a job?"

"Nothing," he said. "It's as dry as a bone out there. I came home to finally tell you."

"Good," she said, smiling and kissing him again.

"Good?" he asked. "It's not good at all. We're about to drop into foreclosure."

"I know," she said. "It won't happen, but I knew."

"How did you know?" he asked, again stunned. "And why won't it happen?"

"Because I am basically rich beyond both our wildest expectations," she said, motioning him to come and join her at the counter. "And that's why I'm glad you didn't find a job because I need you working with me on this now."

"On what?" he asked, feeling more stunned than he had felt in years. He had come home expecting to maybe lose Pam for being so stupid in not telling her about his job. None of what she was saying was making sense.

"I decided I wouldn't tell you what I was doing until you got up the nerve to tell me about the job loss," she said.

"Sorry about that again," he said, his fear again coming back. "I honestly thought I could find another one in a week and not worry about it."

"And then a week turned into a month and then two months, right?" she asked.

"It was killing me," he said. "I didn't want you to think of me as a loser who couldn't even keep a job."

"Pride can make a person really stupid at times," she said, smiling at him.

He could only nod. She wasn't furious, but he could also tell he was a long ways from hearing the end of his idiotic blunder.

"So why are you rich and who exactly is Karl?"

"Karl is one of my bankers," she said. "He's handling the different trusts for me from his bank side."

"You have bankers?" Neil asked. "And trusts?"

"Let me start from the beginning," she said, laughing. "I learned about your job loss about a week after it happened and let me tell you, I was pissed you hadn't told me."

"You had a right to be," he said.

"But that week my Aunt Kelli died and I got distracted."

"You didn't tell me," he said, his voice sounding hollow to his own ears.

"Do you blame me?"

"Not in the slightest."

And he didn't.

"Did I miss her funeral?"

"She didn't have one," Pam said. "Otherwise I would have told you about that."

He nodded. "I'm sorry she's gone. She was a nice person."

"I miss her as well," Pam said. "But we really weren't that close. I just was the only sane one in her family that wasn't after her money, so she gave most of it to me."

"You're kidding? She had money?"

Pam just smiled. "It turned out Aunt Kelli was very rich and I was pretty much her only heir. She mostly cut off her two kids and had already transferred most everything she owned to me in different trusts which became mine at her death."

"How rich was she?" he asked, almost afraid of the answer.

He had liked Aunt Kelli and had been able to make her laugh at times, but he really didn't know that much about her and she had lived in an older home that needed repairs she kept saying she would get around to.

"You know the building you used to work in?" Pam said.

He nodded. It was a seven-story office building in a nice area of town. Modern and expensive.

"It's in one of my trusts. I own it outright, among many other businesses, a small mall, and more apartment buildings than Karl and I can count."

All Neil could do was stare at his wife, his mouth open.

He must still be back in the coffee shop, dreaming. And if he was, he sure didn't want to wake up.

THREE

The next day Pam paid off the entire house mortgage and all the credit cards, erasing in a few phone calls two months of his worry. They went out to dinner to celebrate no debt and being very, very rich.

And the meal was wonderful. They splurged on lobster and the most expensive place in town. It had felt wonderful.

But over the next week it became clear to him very quickly how things were going to be going forward.

He had found a new job. It was working for Pam and the trusts.

It was not their money. It was her money.

She ran the trusts.

She controlled the money.

She just needed him to help her.

The job was right up his alley, actually. He reported to Pam and bossed around a lot of people under him. He managed property and he had an office beside Pam on the top floor of one of her buildings.

But she constantly made it clear that the money was hers, not his.

And he never said a word.

She knew he was a coward and never would say anything.

He had failed, both as a husband in not telling her about his job loss for months and as a business person in not finding a job on his own.

He had proven in a very clear fashion to her that he was a loser. He was useful and she still loved him, but he would never be her real partner in anything again.

Sure, they acted like a married couple and even slept in the same bed and had great sex and laughed and enjoyed each other's company.

He was good for that much at least.

But on the drive home, often alone, he knew the truth.

He had lied to her for months and she had the money and now she was running things.

Period.

And every morning and every evening, driving past those metal beavers on all the mailboxes, he swore they were sneering at him for being such a coward.

For being so stupid.

For being such a loser.

And if they were sneering at him, they were right.

He had made his choice.

He had compromised his last bit of dignity for money and to live in the land of metal beavers.

He deserved whatever look they gave him.

FOUR

It took just under three years before Neil finally had enough.

The day was like any other, warm outside, summer promising soon.

Pam had come into his office, treating him like a secretary, asking why something wasn't done yet.

He had been getting more and more tired of living in her shadow, of feeling worthless. Of all the bosses he had had over the years, she was by far the worst.

By far.

And he had to go home with her every night.

Their marriage was nothing more than a sham and they both knew it. But they never talked about it, just as he had never brought up the fact that he didn't feel like an equal in their marriage.

That's because he wasn't.

And they both knew that as well.

This was her business. He just worked for her.

So after she stood there in the doorway demanding he do something that seemed far, far below his level, he finally clicked over.

The proverbial straw.

He let out a deep sigh and could feel his resolve finally become action and movement.

"I'm going to go home for a time," he said, closing his desk and standing. "I don't feel well."

That stopped her in her tracks. He had never been sick a day in his life and for a moment he actually caught at flash of worry on her face.

"What's wrong?" she asked.

He looked up at her and shook his head. "Somewhere in the last four years I seem to have misplaced my courage, my ability to stand up for myself, my feeling of being worth something. I'm going to go see if I can find it."

He walked around his desk and directly at her where she stood in the door. "Good luck with all this. You should be able to find another flunky easy enough."

He kissed her on the forehead and then pushed past, heading across the reception area for the elevator.

"What are you doing?" she demanded, acting as if she was still in charge of him.

"As I said, I'm going home for a short time to pack a few things."

"You are leaving me?"

She sounded stunned.

"Of course I am," he said, punching the elevator button and then looking back at her angry and surprised look. "What did you expect? I was a man when you married me. Sure, I made a big mistake when I lost my last job, but working like this as your flunky for years is more punishment than I can take."

She stood there, her anger turning to a stunned look on her beautiful face. Clearly she had never thought this day would come. That's how little respect she had for him.

Wow, that was sad.

He really had gotten that pathetic.

"I still love you, Pam," he said as the elevator door slid open and he stepped on. "Enjoy your money. I'll be out of the way by the time you get home."

She said nothing as the elevator doors closed and he turned off his cell phone before he reached the ground floor.

It took him only twenty minutes to pack and fill the back of his paid-off SUV with his stuff. And in the back of his closet he found his guitar. When he pulled it out, his mood soured.

He had stuffed who he really was away for far too long.

She did not show up.

She really didn't think he would go through with this, did she?

He looked at the house, then down the quiet suburban street at the rows of houses that all looked the same and the rows of metal beavers on every mailbox.

God, he had come to hate this place.

But mostly he had come to hate himself.

There was a baseball bat lying on the neighbor's lawn and he went over and picked it up. It felt good in his hands.

Real good.

He moved back over to his mailbox, then with one swing, he smashed the beaver from the top of the box. It went sailing out into the street, the sound echoing down the quiet street.

A surge of excitement went through him, something he hadn't felt in years.

He climbed into the SUV with the bat. His guitar was on the seat beside him.

He rolled down his driver's window.

Then he backed out into the street and gave his house one more look, just as he had given Pam one more look.

Pam would sure be shocked when she got home and he wasn't here waiting for her. She had grown very used to being in charge. This would hurt her ego more than anything.

Then, laughing a real laugh for the first time in years, he turned and headed out of the subdivision, smashing the smirk off of every beaver as he passed.

NEWSLETTER SIGN-UP

Be the first to know!
Just sign up for the Dean Wesley Smith newsletter, and keep up with the latest news, releases and so much more—even the occasional giveaway.

So, what are you waiting for? To sign up go to
deanwesleysmith.com.

But wait! There's more. Sign up for the WMG Publishing newsletter, too, and get the latest news and releases from all of the WMG authors and lines, including Kristine Kathryn Rusch, Kristine Grayson, Kris Nelscott, *Pulphouse Fiction Magazine, Smith's Monthly,* and so much more.
To sign up go to wmgpublishing.com.

ABOUT THE AUTHOR
DEAN WESLEY SMITH

Considered one of the most prolific writers working in modern fiction, with more than 30 million books sold, *USA Today* bestselling writer Dean Wesley Smith published far more than a hundred novels in forty years, and hundreds of short stories across many genres.

At the moment he produces novels in several major series, including the time travel Thunder Mountain novels set in the Old West, the galaxy-spanning Seeders Universe series, the urban fantasy Ghost of a Chance series, a superhero series starring Poker Boy, and a mystery series featuring the retired detectives of the Cold Poker Gang.

His monthly magazine, *Smith's Monthly*, which consists of only his own fiction, premiered in October 2013 and offers readers more than 70,000 words per issue, including a new and original novel every month.

During his career, Dean also wrote a couple dozen *Star Trek* novels, the only two original *Men in Black* novels, Spider-Man and X-Men novels, plus novels set in gaming and television worlds. Writing with his wife Kristine Kathryn Rusch under the name Kathryn Wesley, he wrote the novel for the NBC miniseries The Tenth Kingdom and other books for *Hallmark Hall of Fame* movies.

He wrote novels under dozens of pen names in the worlds of comic books and movies, including novelizations of almost a dozen films, from *The Final Fantasy* to *Steel* to *Rundown*.

Dean also worked as a fiction editor off and on, starting at Pulphouse Publishing, then at *VB Tech Journal*, then Pocket Books, and now at WMG Publishing, where he and Kristine Kathryn Rusch serve as series editors for the acclaimed *Fiction River* anthology series.

For more information about Dean's books and ongoing projects, please visit his website at www.deanwesley-smith.com and sign up for his newsletter.

For more information:
www.deanwesleysmith.com

facebook.com/deanwsmith3
patreon.com/deanwesleysmith
bookbub.com/authors/dean-wesley-smith

EXPANDED COPYRIGHT INFORMATION

"A Long Way Down"
Copyright © 2024 by Dean Wesley Smith
First published in *Smith's Monthly* Issue 31#, April 2016
Published by WMG Publishing
Cover and layout copyright © 2023 by WMG

"A Brush with Intent"
Copyright © 2024 by Dean Wesley Smith
First published in *Smith's Monthly* Issue 54#, December 2016
Cover and layout copyright © 2021 by WMG Publishing
Cover art copyright © Robangel69L/Depositphotos

"A Home for the Books"
Copyright © 2024 by Dean Wesley Smith
First published in *Smith's Monthly* Issue #59, March 2022
Published by WMG Publishing

EXPANDED COPYRIGHT INFORMATION

Cover and layout copyright © 2022 by WMG

"Kill for a Statistic"
Copyright © 2024 by Dean Wesley Smith
First published in *Smith's Monthly* Issue #58, February 2022
Published by WMG Publishing
Cover and layout copyright © 2022 by WMG
Cover art copyright © 2022 GemaIbarra/Depositphotos

"To Remember a Single Minute"
Copyright © 2024 by Dean Wesley Smith
First published in *Stories From July*, WMG Publishing, 2015
Cover design copyright © 2016
WMG Publishing

"A Song for the Old Memory"
Copyright © 2024 by Dean Wesley Smith
First published in *Smith's Monthly* Issue #57, January 2022
Published by WMG Publishing
Cover and layout copyright © 2022 by WMG
Cover art copyright © 2022 sauce7/Depositphotos

"Call Me Unfixable"
Copyright © 2024 by Dean Wesley Smith
First published in *Smith's Monthly* Issue #25, November 2015
Published by WMG Publishing
Cover design copyright © 2015 WMG Publishing

EXPANDED COPYRIGHT INFORMATION

"The Man Who Used Shrill Whispers"
Copyright © 2024 by Dean Wesley Smith
First published in *Smith's Monthly* Issue #37, January 2017
Published by WMG Publishing
Cover design copyright © 2017 WMG Publishing

"An Obscene Crime Against Passion"
Copyright © 2024 by Dean Wesley Smith
First published in Stories From July, WMG Publishing, 2015

"They Were Divided by Cold Debt"
Copyright © 2024 by Dean Wesley Smith
First published in Stories From July, WMG Publishing, 2015